ACK

Nick Warburton was a primary school teacher for ten years before giving up to become a full-time writer. He has written plays for stage and radio, including *Resurrection* and *Conversations from the Engine Room*, which won the 1985 *Radio Times* Drama Award. For young people, he has written *The Thirteenth Owl*, *The Battle of Baked Bean Alley*, *Normal Nesbitt*, *To Trust a Soldier* and *Dennis Dipp on Gilbert's Pond*. A Visiting Fellow of Chichester Institute of Higher Education, he is married with a son and lives in Cambridge.

Books by the same author

Normal Nesbitt
The Thirteenth Owl
To Trust a Soldier

ACKFORD'S MONSTER

NICK WARBURTON

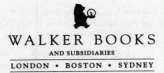

WALKER BOOKS
AND SUBSIDIARIES
LONDON • BOSTON • SYDNEY

For Mary Waters

*Special thanks to the Edinburgh team:
Lesley, Steve, Amanda, Clare, Chris,
Nicky-Jane and Janet*

N.W.

First published 1996 by Walker Books Ltd
87 Vauxhall Walk, London SE11 5HJ

This edition published 1996

2 4 6 8 10 9 7 5 3

Text © 1996 Nick Warburton
Cover illustration © 1996 Stuart Bodek

This book has been typeset in Sabon.

Printed in England

British Library Cataloguing in Publication Data
A catalogue record for this book is available from
the British Library.

ISBN 0-7445-4752-0

CONTENTS

A WAVE FROM NOWHERE

The monster came to them on the day of the funeral. The summer of 1914.

They stood at the graveside in St Peter's churchyard, with their heads bowed and Hannah could hear the distant sea, breathing like a tired old man.

It was another hot day. She looked down and saw dust on their boots. Hers and Elizabeth's and Judith's. They ought to be clean and shiny, she thought, for Daddy's sake, but you couldn't keep the dust off.

The new rector said his last prayer very softly, almost a whisper. Hannah could hear every word, though, because the air was so still.

In the name of the Father, and of the Son...

She lifted her head and looked at the little group in their best dark clothes. Her father had been a quiet man. He'd kept himself to himself. Not many people from Ackford had come to pay their last respects. Hannah was glad of that. She didn't want too many people about.

She saw Mrs Corbiss from the cottage next door, with her eyes tight shut. Two of the fishermen from the village, William and his son David, who used to go out with her father in the boat. Her big sister Elizabeth. Straight black hair under her black bonnet. A pale, sad face. Elizabeth would have to look after them all now.

And Judith. The middle daughter. The troublesome one.

Judith had her blue eyes wide open, looking hard at the open grave. Her fair hair tied back. She wouldn't wear a hat because she said her father had liked to see her hair.

"Daddy," she said in a thin, clear voice. "Daddy."

Hannah saw Mrs Corbiss jerk her head up in surprise. Elizabeth stretched out a hand and touched Judith's arm but Judith didn't seem to feel it. She turned her back on the grave and began to walk away. It was the first funeral Hannah had ever been to, but she knew you weren't supposed to do that.

Judith walked straight through the churchyard, past overgrown graves, down the slope towards the small back gate. The rector took a step towards her and stopped. He didn't know what to do next.

"Miss Richards…" he said uncertainly to Elizabeth. "Should we … I mean, shall I… ?"

Elizabeth tightened her lips and turned to Hannah.

"Stay here, Hannah," she said. "Stay with the rector."

She began to follow Judith, trying not to hurry. Hannah looked at the rector, at his puzzled face and his jutting ears, and knew she didn't want to stay with him. He hadn't known Daddy. He didn't even have a name she could call him by. This was nothing to do with him and she wanted to be with her sisters.

Judith had walked along the sea path towards the cottage. Then down the shelf of stones towards the sea itself. The stones rolled and clicked under her boots but she didn't stumble. She held herself upright and looked straight ahead, like someone walking in her sleep. Elizabeth had stopped halfway down the beach.

"Judith," she called. "Come back."

But Judith walked on until she came to the very edge. Line after line of flat waves faded into the shingle and sucked back into the sea. They trickled over her boots and pulled at the hem of her skirt.

Hannah stood at the top of the beach, watching, squinting against the sun hanging over the water. She saw a shimmer of white light on the wet shingle. She heard the grate of feet on stones and guessed that the rector and the others were standing behind her.

Judith moved on, into the water.

She lifted her arms, holding them out as if she wanted to cling to someone. But there was only the wide, flat sea before her. The water lapped round her waist and darkened against her blouse. And still she walked on.

"Daddy," Hannah heard her cry. "Daddy, Daddy, Daddy!"

Crying like a gull, piercing the air, lonely.

And then the sea seemed to heave and sink.

A wave is lifting her, Hannah thought. A big wave from nowhere on a calm sea.

A glistening rock broke the surface in front of Judith. Clinging weed on a brown-green rock out of nowhere. Lifting slowly out of the water. It rose and the sea spilled off it in white streams. And it seemed to change shape. It was not a rock but a moving thing. Swaying from side to side. A boulder-like head and round shoulders. Everything was silent and still for a moment. Only the waves tugging at Judith's skirt and the water falling in little streams off this rock-thing.

Then it began to move towards her.

The silence was broken. Elizabeth screamed and started to run. Hannah wanted to run, too, but she felt Mrs Corbiss's hand grip her elbow. All around her, stones were rattling and the rector and William were sliding past her down the slope of the beach.

"Daddy, Daddy, Daddy!" Judith was crying, with her head back and her face to the sky.

And the thing, the creature like a rock, made a moaning sound, deep like the wind in the church tower. Hannah saw something dark and gnarled lift above Judith's head. A length of raw bone or driftwood, but alive.

The sea foamed and Judith twisted sideways, her arms flailing in the water.

David ran by Hannah, dragging something that fanned out behind him and swished on the shingle. A net.

The two men and David strode into the sea. William lifted a stone and brought it down on the creature. And again. Clubbing it. Hannah couldn't tell whether he was hitting head or back or shoulder. She closed her eyes and turned her head away.

Then David flung the net. It curved through the air, billowed and dropped, and he fell backwards as he tried to pull it tight.

The rector took Judith in his arms and began to wade out of the sea with her. She hung from his arms, her yellow hair spreading in the water. He carried her a little way up the beach and then stumbled to his knees, shaking his head and choking. Elizabeth knelt beside her and held her pale face between her hands.

At first Hannah thought she was dead. She thought Judith was dead. Then she saw her curl up and cling on to Elizabeth's skirt.

William and David hauled the black shape of the net out of the water. It came grating and sucking against the pull of the little waves. The thing inside it rolled and dragged, lifeless and heavy.

"Please, Mrs Corbiss," Hannah said, "let me go to her."

Mrs Corbiss's hand stayed tight around her arm but she walked with her to where Elizabeth was holding Judith. Elizabeth looked up at Hannah and her face was wet with tears and seawater.

"Mrs Corbiss," the rector said, his voice trembling. "It is Mrs Corbiss, isn't it?"

"Yes, rector."

"Will you help, Mrs Corbiss? Help Elizabeth with her sister."

Mrs Corbiss let go of Hannah's elbow and stepped back a little.

"I don't know, rector. I don't know she'd want me to."

"Of course she does. I'm going to take her back to the cottage. You help Elizabeth, Mrs Corbiss. Please."

He gathered Judith in his arms again and began to walk towards the line of spiky grass at the top of the beach. Elizabeth and Mrs Corbiss followed him, side by side, without a glance between them, not speaking.

Hannah turned round and saw William and his son standing over the dark bulk they'd trapped in the net. William wiped his face with the crook of his arm. Then he lifted his foot and pushed it against the thing in the net. It lolled over, unfolding, as big as a donkey she'd once seen in a ditch. Part of the net fell aside and, suddenly, Hannah could see what it was that had come to her sister out of the sea.

A HAND, A CLAW

She saw a kind of hand, clawed up as if it were
grasping something. There were knuckles, and
small hooked nails, and webbing between the
grey fingers. It rested on the round boulder of
the creature's head, like some long-dead
animal, like a dead toad you might see by the
roadside.

It's trying to keep the light out, Hannah
thought.

A hand. A claw.

A tangle of hair or seaweed covered the
body; long strands of it, knotted thick as
bindweed stems, but dark and slimy. Some
were almost orange in colour and some dark
brown. Hannah couldn't tell whether they
belonged to the body or whether they were
plants growing on it.

It was disgusting, ugly. Hannah was nearly
sick at the sight of it, but she couldn't look away.

Then she saw its fingers clench a little and heard a bubbling hiss of air.

"Still alive," said William, stepping back at the sound.

Hannah stepped back, too. David dropped a corner of the net and looked up at his father. His face was smooth and pale.

"What'll we do, Dad?" he said.

"Don't know. Don't know what we'll do."

"It came to Judith," Hannah said.

William turned, surprised to see her there.

"I know, missy."

He stooped quickly, scrabbled among the larger stones till he found one to fill his palm, and then straightened.

"We'd best kill it," he said.

Best kill it.

Take its life, like her father's life had been taken from him.

Hannah thought about her father again and almost cried.

When this thing had come out of the sea, it had stopped her thinking about him. She'd thought about him all day long till then. She'd thought about him when she woke, knowing straightaway it was the day they were to bury him. And she'd thought about him, remembering him, every minute after that.

What she remembered most was him taking his spade from the little shed at the back of the

15

cottage and walking out to dig for early potatoes. She remembered his back blocking the light at the kitchen door. Then taking up the spade and walking away. He hated digging. He was a fisherman. He wasn't easy on the land.

Hannah remembered this most of all because it was the last time she'd seen him alive.

And now he was dead and this creature was alive.

This creature that had stopped her thinking about her daddy.

Why should that be? Why should some ugly creature be alive while my daddy is dead?

Yes. It was best to kill it. She could've found a stone and killed it herself.

"William!"
The rector was hurrying down the beach towards them. William had one leg braced and the stone poised above his head. When he heard the rector's voice he hesitated, then let the weight of the stone swing his arm down loose. He looked at the creature in the net, waiting for the rector to reach them.

"She'll be all right," the rector said as he ran up. He was breathing hard through his teeth. "She's had a fright ... a bad fright ... but I don't think she's been harmed."

William said nothing. The stone swung a

little at his side. The rector glanced at it and looked away again.

He still doesn't know what to do, Hannah thought. He can't be more than a year or two older than Judith. His cheeks are pink and his ears stick out. How can he know what we ought to do?

"Do you know what it is, William?" he asked.

"No, sir."

"Have you seen anything like it before?"

"No, sir. Not in forty years. I don't think I wants to see anything else like it, either."

"No. I'm sure."

The rector dropped on his haunches and rested his elbows on his knees. He linked his fingers, tapping them against his chin, thinking. For several moments nobody spoke. Then he stretched out a hand and lifted the corner of the net. He put his head on one side to get a better look at the creature.

Hannah had seen people look like that before. Peering into prams, curious to get a glimpse of a new baby.

"I don't think we need to…" he said at last, almost to himself.

"Need to what, mister?"

"I mean, I think we ought to consider before we do anything else."

"What is there to consider, then?" William asked.

"You mustn't ... I don't think we should kill it. That's all."

He was squinting up at William, balancing on his heels with the sun full on his face. Hannah suddenly felt that she wanted to push him. Push him over so he'd sprawl on the beach and look ridiculous.

"Take it up to the cottages, will you?"

William narrowed his eyes and set his mouth. He wanted what Hannah wanted but he couldn't argue with a man of God.

"What shall we do with it up there?"

"Find somewhere to secure it. There's a pig-sty, isn't there?" said the rector. He turned to Hannah. "Isn't there a pig-sty up there, little girl?"

Little girl.

Hannah nodded.

"Then see that it's put in there. We'll get someone to watch over it. But it must not be harmed, William. We must do it no harm until we've had time to consider."

William sighed and dropped his stone. He wouldn't tell the rector what he thought. He'd keep it to himself and do as he was told.

If I was a man... Hannah thought fiercely ...

She stooped and snatched up a handful of pebbles. Then she flung them wildly, not caring where they went. The rector flinched and raised his elbow. Most of the pebbles went skittering harmlessly over the beach, jumping off at all angles. Some thudded into the wet mound at the rector's feet and stuck there.

The creature's fingers twitched against its head, but it made no other movement.

She clicked the latch and pushed open the kitchen door but didn't go in. She didn't like to because she didn't know what she would find. The only thing she was sure of was that Daddy wouldn't be there.

Briefly she looked at the door; at the wood rubbed grey by the winds off the sea, and the heavy nails holding the crosspieces in place. Then she looked into the kitchen.

Judith was asleep in the old armchair by the empty fireplace. Her face was white and her yellow hair was flat and damp against her head. Hannah thought how frightened she looked, even asleep, and how small. Frightened to smallness.

"Ssh."

Elizabeth, with one hand on the kettle, gestured to Hannah to keep quiet. Mrs Corbiss sat stiffly watching Hannah, her arms folded and her black bonnet on the kitchen table in front of her. She was sitting in Daddy's place.

Hannah squirmed under Mrs Corbiss's firm gaze and looked quickly away. She fixed her eyes on the mantelpiece behind the old woman. On Daddy's old tin box.

That morning, before the funeral, Elizabeth had taken the dull grey box down and held it out for Hannah to see.

"There's some of Daddy's precious things in here, Han," she'd said. "One of them's for you to keep. You'd like one of Daddy's treasures to keep for always, wouldn't you?"

Of course she would. Elizabeth shouldn't have asked like that, talking to her as if she were a little girl again.

"It'll cost you nothing but a promise. I'll tell you about it when we get back from the church."

Hannah had imagined them returning to the cottage, walking back into the emptiness Daddy had left, and opening the box to find something he had owned, some part of him. What happened on the beach had changed all that.

"Well, Hannah," Mrs Corbiss was saying in a low voice, "what are they doing out there?"

"Carrying it up to the pigsty. He says they're not to kill it."

Mrs Corbiss pinched the peppery skin of her face together, like a fist clenching.

"I thought better of William than that," she said. "What's the use of bringing it up here?"

"William was going to kill it but he said—"

"He?"

"The rector. He said there was things to consider first."

"He doesn't know day from night, that man. I thought that at the burial."

Elizabeth put the kettle on the range and came to sit at the table. She picked at the ribbons of Mrs Corbiss's bonnet, twisting them in her fingers. Then she sighed and put her hands in her lap. Hannah stayed by the open door, watching. She pressed her back against it and heard it creak a little.

"Stand still, child," said Mrs Corbiss quietly.

"I am to be the mother here now, Mrs Corbiss," Elizabeth said. "I shall have to take care of these two."

"Of course you are, Elizabeth. It was the same for me when my Corbiss was taken. God will give you strength."

"I won't come running to you all the time. But ... I don't know what to do about this."

She lifted her head and looked across the kitchen at Judith.

"I don't understand what's happened. What shall I do?"

"Do? What is there to do?"

"About Judith, and what happened to her. I must—"

"You must carry on, Elizabeth. That's the first thing, and the main one. The creature must be killed. And then you must carry on."

"How can it be killed if the rector's said leave it?"

"Oh," said Mrs Corbiss, "you can't let him have the last word."

"Then what…"

Mrs Corbiss gave Elizabeth a look which silenced her. Hannah saw the old woman's small black eyes glint like the nails in the door.

"We shall go up to the castle," Mrs Corbiss said firmly. "You and me, Elizabeth. We'll see Major Bartholomew. He can outsay the rector. Don't you worry about that."

TO THE CASTLE

"I was under the water," Judith said. "I was breathing it in. Green and gold water, just like air."

Hannah was kneeling on the rug with her chin on the soft arm of the chair. She took Judith's hand and held it to her cheek.

"You nearly drowned, Jude," she said.

"No. It wasn't that. It was sweet. It was like walking through the orchard with the sun coming through the blossom. You know, how the air is kept warm. I wasn't frightened."

"That was a dream," Elizabeth said in her matter-of-fact voice. She had her back to her sisters and was busying herself at the sink.

"Yes," said Judith. "A dream."

Daddy had always said that Judith was the dreamy one. Sometimes she would tell Hannah her dreams, turning them into stories for her. Her dreams were full of beautiful light and strange, nameless ladies and gentlemen, not Ackford people, who led her into flowery places and said things that sounded like poetry. When Hannah dreamed she saw ordinary folk doing almost ordinary things. Once she dreamed that Mrs Corbiss was walking down the lane to church with a mouse in a bottle. And another time she saw Daddy spinning a net out over the sea like one of the disciples. That was odd because Daddy always fished from his boat, not standing on the shore, but it was really too ordinary to turn into a story. In fact, she dreamed such ordinary dreams that she hardly ever remembered them. But Judith's stories she told herself over and over, until she felt they were her own.

"Do you remember what happened?" Hannah asked.

"What happened?"

"Down on the beach?"

Judith frowned and looked into the distance.

"I walked into the water," she said slowly. "And I was calling for Daddy."

"And then a creature came out of the water…"

"Daddy? Was Daddy there?"

"No, Jude. It was an ugly monster and it—"

"Hannah," said Elizabeth sharply. She came over from the sink, wiping her hands on a cloth. "Judith is tired. You won't help by reminding her."

"I was only asking…"

"Well, don't. It's not kind."

"I remember what I was thinking," Judith said. "Daddy was a fisherman and we buried him in the ground."

"Of course we did."

"But he loved the sea, Elizabeth…"

"We did what we had to do. We did what was best. We took him to St Peter's, to be with God."

Elizabeth smiled sadly and sat on the arm of the chair. She put her hand on Judith's brow. Hannah loved that moment, the three of them together at the old chair. It was almost as if their daddy was busy in the next room, and might come in to see them at any moment.

"I think you should try to sleep," Elizabeth said.

Then the sound of hammering started up outside, the flat echoing of iron on planks. And a gruff voice shouting instructions. Judith opened her eyes wide.

"What's that?"

"Just some of the men from the village," Elizabeth said, stroking her hair. "Nothing to fret about."

"What are they doing?"

"Nothing much." Elizabeth looked at Hannah and gave a silent shake of her head.

Say nothing. "They're doing some work on the pigsty. Will they keep you awake?"

But Judith had already fallen asleep again.

The path to the castle was wide enough for two if they walked close together. Hannah didn't want to walk beside Mrs Corbiss so she remained a pace or two behind, skipping now and then to keep up with her.

"Where's Elizabeth?" the old woman asked.

"With Jude. She didn't want to leave her."

"Why couldn't you stay behind?"

"Because I talk too much."

"Talk too much?" snorted Mrs Corbiss. "You barely say a word, girl."

"Elizabeth's told me what to say, when we get to the castle."

"No, Hannah. You say nothing. Leave the saying to me. You just come as one of the family."

The castle was very old, and worn to an unevenness by the weather. It seemed to be leaning into the wind, and it jutted there off its small green hill like an old tooth. At least, that's how it looked to Hannah when she saw it from the beach. Close to it was a different matter. Sombre and weighty. She imagined that it reached deep into the ground, that there were heavy walls and rooms down there in the darkness. Of course, Hannah had never been inside the castle. She had never wanted to. She was only going now because she felt that, somehow, she would be helping Judith and Elizabeth. And because Mrs Corbiss was leading the way.

The moat was dry. No one in Ackford could remember a time when it held water. Since the soldiers had come, though, it had been filled with coils of barbed wire and wooden stakes carved to rough points. There was a narrow bridge over this ugly hedge of posts and wire, and Mrs Corbiss walked boldly over it. Her boots clattered on the planks and brought a sentry to his feet. He had been kneeling down with his back to them, trying to flick matches into a tin mug.

"What's up here?" he asked, barring Mrs Corbiss's way.

His tunic was unbuttoned at the neck and there was an uncertain, almost frightened expression on his sweaty face. Mrs Corbiss stopped in front of him.

"We've come to see Major Bartholomew," she said.

"What for?"

"That's for him to know."

"Then tell me and I'll tell him."

"That I shan't."

She folded her arms and looked doggedly up at him. Hannah knew that she would not move off the little bridge until she had her way.

* * *

Hannah put out her hand to steady herself as they spiralled slowly upwards. The stone was cool beneath her fingers, the air blotchy and dark. After the glare outside, she found it hard to see her way and her feet stumbled against wedged steps. She could hear Mrs Corbiss breathing through her nose a little way behind her. Eventually they climbed into a circular chamber where light streamed in through window slits.

"Wait here," said the soldier, and he crossed to a door, knocked, and went in.

Hannah glanced at Mrs Corbiss, wanting to say something to her, but the old woman stood there stoutly, squinting across the room at nothing. After a moment the soldier put his head out of the door and called them over.

"You can have ten minutes," he said. "The Major is a busy man."

Major Bartholomew sat at a heavy desk, a dark shape surrounded by light from the narrow window behind him. Hannah could make out nothing of his features until she moved a little to one side. Then she saw a slight, round-faced man with grey eyes behind steel-rimmed spectacles. He was looking at them over linked fingers.

On the desk in front of him was a jamjar half-filled with cloudy water. There were brushes on the desk, and a battered tin of watercolours.

"What can I do for you?" he said, and smiled.

He had a nice face, Hannah thought. His tunic was also unbuttoned at the neck, and his cuffs were folded back to expose thin wrists. Stripes of green and brown paint marked his hands.

Mrs Corbiss half-turned to indicate Hannah.

"This is one of the Richards girls," she said. "They have a cottage next to mine, down along the shore."

"I see," said Major Bartholomew, and waited.

"I've come to see you because of the trouble they've run into."

"Trouble? I'm sorry to hear that, Miss Richards."

He looked at Hannah and she lowered her eyes.

"The soldiers are here for our protection, Major. Isn't that so?" Mrs Corbiss went on.

"Well, in a sense, yes. Though, strictly speaking, they are here to watch the coast, Mrs..."

"Corbiss."

"They are here to watch the coast, Mrs Corbiss. I don't think there's any secret about that. You know that we live in troubled times, that there are developments in Europe..."

"I know that, yes."

29

"...and that, well, to be honest with you, this stretch of coast may be quite vulnerable..."

"Yes, Major. It's that I've come about."

"The coast?"

"Possibly."

Major Bartholomew breathed deeply and stood up. He was much taller than he'd seemed behind his desk. He walked to the window and looked out. Hannah tried to see what he had been painting. Some sort of landscape: long grass bending in the wind, a river opening flatly into the sea.

"You have some information, perhaps, Mrs Corbiss," he said.

"Maybe so. It's hard to say."

"So it seems. All the same, if you know of any movements—"

"We have taken a creature out of the sea," said Mrs Corbiss suddenly.

He turned from the window and frowned with amusement at her.

"A creature?"

"Which threatened this girl's sister."

"What sort of creature?"

"I can't say. Like nothing I've seen before. We caught it in a net."

"A fish, you mean?"

"No, Major. Not a fish."

"What then? A seal?"

"Of course not. More human than fish or seal."

"A man?"

"A creature. I hardly saw it myself."

"What about you, Miss Richards? Did you see it?"

"Yes," said Hannah quietly.

"And what did you think it was?"

She sucked her lower lip and recalled the tangle of glistening stems, orange and brown, and its heavy head on the beach.

"A monster, sir," she said. "Judith walked into the sea and … it came for her."

"It came for her? You're sure?"

"Yes," said Mrs Corbiss. "Only we got to her first."

"And is she all right?"

"As far as we can tell."

"Extraordinary," Major Bartholomew said to himself.

For a while he stared out of the window and Mrs Corbiss studied the back of his head. Short hair, black and shiny, with a ridge where he wore his cap. Then he sat down at his desk again and spoke briskly.

"What you tell me is quite extraordinary, Mrs Corbiss, but I don't see what it has to do with me. I mean, is it really a military matter? It was caught in your nets, you say?"

"That's right."

"Well, what do you usually do with what you catch in your nets?"

"Sell it, sir. Or eat it."

31

"In that case…"

"Eat it, Major?"

"No, no, I suppose not. But, well, I'm at a loss to suggest…"

"You said yourself, Major Bartholomew, you're here to watch the coast. To look out for movements. And this thing comes along, and it's most certainly what I would call suspicious."

"I see."

"And that is likely to be a military matter, isn't it?"

"I see, I see."

"Only, the rector says we're not to kill it. So, what do you think, Major Bartholomew? Will you come down to the cottages and see for yourself?"

FLOWERS
ON THE SEA

Early the following morning, Hannah walked round the side of the cottage and made her way to the beach. At least, she pretended to herself that that was what she was doing. When she saw the pigsty, though, she stopped and suddenly knew she meant to go no further.

David was sitting on the pigsty wall with a pitchfork across his knees. His head was lolling on his chest. He was a sturdy boy and he had a way of flicking his dark hair out of his eyes that somehow made him look grown up. He was proud of the fact that his birthday was a clear month before Hannah's, and that he often went out in the boats with William, but to her he still seemed quite young. Especially now, sitting asleep on the wall, puffing out his smooth cheeks.

She watched him for a while and then took a step or two towards him, deliberately scraping her boots on the stone slabs. David's head jerked up and he sprang off the wall, stumbling awkwardly.

"I was told to watch," he mumbled. "I'm meant to be here."

"I know that," said Hannah. "What's it doing?"

He glanced over his shoulder at the pigsty.

"Nothing. It doesn't move much."

"Is it alive?"

"Yes. You want to look?"

"No," she said at once, stepping away and putting her hands behind her back.

"It can't get out," David said with a little smile. "And I've got this."

He tossed the pitchfork from hand to hand.

Hannah followed him through the gap in the wall into the empty pig run. They shuffled through wisps of dry, grey straw and Hannah breathed in the warm, yeasty smell of chicken-feed. There were no pigs in the run now, and hadn't been for more than a year. Their place had been taken by a clutch of dusty brown hens who came and went as they pleased.

The hens pleased not to be around this morning, Hannah noticed. She could neither see nor hear them.

The sty was a low stone shed in a corner of the run. Someone had nailed planks to the posts across the entrance and propped poles against them to hold them firm. It looked a hurried job, but very secure.

She tried to peer through the gaps between the planks. Nothing there but shadow.

"You have to get closer to see anything," said David, and when she hesitated he grinned and nodded.

"You don't have to worry. It'll be all right."

She edged closer, and stooped.

At first she could make out nothing at all, but then patches of shadow seemed to move slightly, rubbing silently against each other.

Yes. It was there.

She saw something settle and slump. A sagging weight of some kind of dark flesh. And those twisting, weedy fronds. She stayed there for some moments, hardly breathing. Turning her head slightly, she checked that David was still close by with his pitchfork.

She thought she could detect something different about the creature. It didn't look exactly as it had done on the beach. There was no claw covering its head. She saw a black hole, like a post hole in soft ground, filled with rain. A wet, dark hole.

Its eye. Open and staring.

Then a thin screeching sound cut through the air and Hannah's heart jumped. She leapt back and knocked into David, who was already turning for the gap in the wall.

"Hannah!"

It was Elizabeth's voice. Screaming at her.

"Hannah! What are you doing there?"

Elizabeth was hurrying towards the pigsty, her black hair flying from side to side. She grabbed Hannah by the wrist and her nails dug in hard.

"What do you think you're doing?"

"I only wanted to—"

"And you," Elizabeth snapped at David. "Why didn't you stop her?"

"But it's all right," David said slowly. "It can't do no harm."

"Don't be so stupid! Can't do no harm. You saw it yourself, you crack-brain!"

"But it's safe enough…"

"Shut up! Shut up!"

She jerked on Hannah's wrist and pulled her close. Hannah felt her face crushed into Elizabeth's stiff black blouse. A button was pressing into her cheek and she thought she was going to cry, though she didn't know why.

For a while none of them spoke. Elizabeth had her arms tight around Hannah, rocking her gently. David stood apart and looked miserably at the ground. That's how Major Bartholomew found them when he came round the side of the cottage a moment later.

"Good morning," he called cheerfully. 'Mrs Corbiss said I might find you here."

Elizabeth released Hannah and smoothed down the front of her apron.

"You'd be Major Bartholomew?" she said.

"Indeed, yes. I've come to see … well, to see what's what."

He caught sight of David's pitchfork and raised his eyebrows.

"I say, how deadly. You're on sentry duty, I take it?"

David straightened and grinned at him but didn't answer.

"I hope you're prepared to use that thing," Major Bartholomew said with a smile. "*In extremis.*"

"Oh yes, sir."

"Good, good. That must be a comfort to the ladies."

He switched off his smile and glanced in the direction of the pigsty. Removing his glasses he pinched the bridge of his long nose between thumb and forefinger.

"I assume the … creature is in there, is it?" he asked.

"Yes, sir. I was just saying, it's quite safe for the present. It doesn't move much."

"Splendid. I'm relieved to hear it."

"Would you like to come in, Major Bartholomew," Elizabeth said. "I'll get some tea on."

"Thank you, yes. You go ahead, Miss Richards. I'll just see what there is to see out here and then I'll join you, if I may."

* * *

37

Elizabeth bustled Hannah into tidying the kitchen and taking one of the best cups from the top shelf of the dresser.

"And a saucer, Han," she said briskly. "What'll he think if we just give him a cup?"

Hannah was pleased to be busy. It meant they didn't have to talk about what had happened in the yard; about her own foolishness and the way her quiet, sensible sister had screamed at her, such a strange, unearthly scream. It also meant she could push to the back of her mind what she had seen in the pigsty. The creature's dark pit of a watching eye.

In the days after her Daddy had died, Hannah had found it was best to keep busy. She'd found small jobs to do and done them with energy and purpose. They hadn't blotted out thoughts of him entirely, she hadn't wanted them to do that, but they'd somehow eased the pain a little.

By the time Major Bartholomew appeared, stooping, at the kitchen door, the kettle was humming on the range and a chair had been placed at the table ready for him.

"First of all," he said as he sat down, "I should say how sorry I was to hear about your father."

"Thank you, sir. It's a great loss but we shall bear it."

"I'm sure."

"He would want us to."

He spread his hands on the table and studied them.

"I did meet him, in fact. I make it my business to speak to all the fishermen in Ackford. I regard them as our ears and eyes. He seemed to me a good man."

"He was, sir," said Elizabeth. "An upright and a God-fearing man."

He gave a little sympathetic twitch, not quite a smile, and then continued in a business-like tone.

"With regard to this creature... Well, I'm not sure what to think, to be honest with you. Your young sentry showed me the sty, but I could make little of it. I mean, I couldn't really see. It appeared to be quite human in some respects, but not entirely so. Your neighbour, Mrs Corbiss, wants me to do something about it, though I'm not sure what."

"She wants what we all want, Major," said Elizabeth.

"And that is?"

"To have it killed."

"Killed. I see."

He drummed his fingers lightly on the table. Hannah watched him from her quiet place behind the armchair. She thought he looked troubled at the thought. Mrs Corbiss had told him the same thing yesterday, she remembered, but he seemed to have forgotten.

"It must have been a terrible experience for you," he said.

"It was."

"Though … forgive me if this sounds unfeeling, but you appear to have survived remarkably well…"

"I have?"

"Thank heavens that you have. But…"

"It was my sister he attacked, Major. Judith. She's asleep upstairs."

"Oh, I'm sorry. I didn't…"

"And I wouldn't say that she had survived so well. She's not so well at all, in fact."

"Your sister? I'm sorry."

"We would've done it ourselves, too," Elizabeth went on. "Killed the beast ourselves. Only the rector says we mustn't do that."

"Yes. Perhaps I should talk to him."

"Do you really need to do that? If you think…"

"But I don't know what I think, Miss Richards. That's the trouble."

"We don't want it here. Dead or alive."

"Yes, I can appreciate that."

Elizabeth went to the kettle to make the tea. Major Bartholomew sighed and ran his fingers through his hair. Then he looked up and caught sight of Hannah.

"I see," he said, smiling at her. "There are three Miss Richards. I shall get into muddles if I call you all Miss Richards. What other names do you have?"

"I'm Hannah. This is Elizabeth."

"And Judith who is asleep. Of course. I see. May I call you by those names, do you think?"

Hannah looked at her sister as she carried the teapot to the table. That was something for Elizabeth to decide.

"Of course, Major Bartholomew," Elizabeth said. "But can you tell us what you mean to do about the monster? I can't get things straight until it's all cleared up."

"Of course, of course," he said with sudden purpose. "You must be clear in your mind, and I'll do what I can."

"Thank you, sir."

"To begin with," he said, "I shall have it moved to the castle. I think that's probably the first step to take, don't you?"

He smiled from Hannah to Elizabeth, and Hannah saw her sister purse her lips in disappointment as she poured the milk into his cup.

Judith woke just before midday and came downstairs in her nightgown. She stood on the bottom step, blinking and holding on to the stairway door with a pale hand. The sunlight streamed down the stairs behind her, shining through her fair hair and the edges of her white gown. Hannah had been frowning with concentration while she polished a strap of horse brasses at the table. At the sound of the latch she'd looked up and suddenly thought how like an angel Judith looked. She felt a brief pang, part pride and part jealousy.

"Why didn't you wake me?" Judith asked.

"You need to sleep," said Elizabeth. "You shouldn't come down like that, Jude. We've had visitors."

"Visitors?"

"Major Bartholomew."

"Why?"

"There are things to talk about, that's all. Are you getting up, or do you want to sleep on?"

"I've had enough of sleep," said Judith.

"Then go and get dressed."

"I know. I don't need to be told."

Judith turned and went back upstairs. Elizabeth hurried over to the table and sat down close to Hannah. She took the cloth and the strap from her hands and put them down.

"The soldiers are coming this afternoon," she said quietly. "They're taking the monster up to the castle."

"I know."

"Listen to me, Hannah. I don't want Judith to be here when they come. Will you take her out for a walk? Will you do that for me?"

"She might not want to. I can't make her…"

"No," said Elizabeth, sighing a little and thinking hard. "Tell her you want to go out.

Ask her to take you somewhere."

"Where?"

"It doesn't matter. St Peter's. To see Daddy's grave."

Hannah stared at her sister's urgent, imploring face as she leaned across the table. She wasn't sure that she wanted to see the grave, even to save Judith from another encounter with the monster. She wasn't sure that she wanted to be reminded that Daddy was up there and would never return. But she didn't want to be around when the soldiers came for the monster either.

"She might go to see Daddy's grave," Elizabeth whispered. "If you ask her right."

"I'll try," said Hannah.

"You're a good girl, Han."

Elizabeth gave her a quick smile and squeezed her cheek. Then she hurried up the stairs after Judith. As Hannah put away her cloths and hung the horse brasses back by the fireplace, she heard her sisters talking upstairs: Elizabeth, low and insistent, and, after a while, Judith, sharp and angry.

"Don't," she said out loud to herself. "Don't argue. There's nothing to argue about."

She had no trouble persuading Judith to go for a walk. Judith didn't want to stay in anyway.

"Not with her," she said darkly. "Telling

me what I ought to do."

"Will you come up to the church with me, then?" Hannah asked, hoping that Judith would suggest somewhere else. Into Ackford, up to the castle. Anywhere but the church. But Judith's eyes flashed and she said, "Yes, Han. Let's go to the church. Just you and me."

They found the fresh mound of dry yellow earth but neither of them felt that it meant very much. It was just another plot among the leaning headstones and the tufts of coarse grass. Nothing to do with Daddy. They picked some flowers and left them there, but Judith said it would have been better to scatter them on the sea.

"Perhaps we can do that tomorrow," Hannah suggested.

"Yes," said Judith. Her face was angry and beautiful as she stared down at the grave. "That'll give us something to look forward to."

"There's nothing else we can do, though, Jude. Is there?"

"What do you mean?"

"There's nothing we can do for Daddy now. It's too late, isn't it?"

And suddenly there was a rim of water in Hannah's eyes, and the flowers on the untidy grave began to twist and swirl. She sighed shakily and tried to sniff.

"Oh, Han," said Judith, taking hold of Hannah's useless hands. "Sit down a moment."

Hannah sank to her knees and pressed her sister's hands in her lap.

"I don't know, Jude," she said. "I want to do something for Daddy but I don't know what. And I think I'm too small and young ... and there's nothing ... nothing I can do..."

"Don't think that, Hannah. Of course there's something you can do."

"But what?"

"I don't know. I hardly know what to do myself. But you'll find something. And when you do you'll know it'll be right."

"Elizabeth knows already. She can take care of the cottage for us and..."

"You mustn't think you're too little to help. Daddy will want you to do something. And it'll be just as good as what Elizabeth does, or what I do."

"Yes," said Hannah on a deep breath. "But I want it to be something real."

"It will be, Han. Of course it will."

On their way out of the churchyard they met the new rector.

"I'm pleased to see you up and about," he told Judith.

He smiled nervously at her and didn't seem to notice Hannah at all. Judith looked steadily at him but said nothing. Red patches appeared

45

on his cheeks and he turned away, screwing up his eyes and seeming to spot something of interest in the distant trees.

"If I can be of any assistance…" he said eventually, and trailed off into awkward silence.

"I'm sure Elizabeth thinks you can," Judith said. "Doesn't she?"

"I'm sorry. I don't understand…"

"No? Well, we'll see, won't we?"

They left him standing helplessly at the churchyard gate. Hannah felt his gaze following them as they walked quickly down the path towards the sea. They entered a tunnel of overhanging trees.

The meeting had taken the softness out of Judith again. She walked stiffly ahead of Hannah and bent to pick up a stick and swish irritably at the long grass with it.

"If I can be of any assistance," she muttered. "How can he be any use at all? He's hardly more than a boy."

"And his ears stick out," said Hannah. "Did you notice?"

"Ha! Yes. Yes, they do. Flap, flap, flap."

She scythed at the grass again and then hurled the stick clattering into the trees. They walked on without speaking for a while, and then Hannah asked, "Does Elizabeth like him, though?"

"What?"

"You said Elizabeth thinks the rector might help. Has she been speaking to him, do you think?"

Hannah was looking down at her feet, trying to tread exactly where her sister had, when she suddenly saw that Judith had stopped and turned round. She had to put her hand on Judith's arm to prevent herself stumbling. For a second or two they were face to face on the path.

"Has she, then?" Hannah said softly. "Been speaking to the rector?"

Judith looked down at her without answering.

"I'd like to go to the beach, Han," she said at last. "Do you mind?"

"Of course not. Let's do that."

"By myself, I mean. I want to be by myself for a bit."

"Oh. Yes. I don't mind."

Hannah turned and made her way slowly homewards. The sea was spread out on her right, flat and dull, and there was dullness aching inside her, too. A kind of longing to make some gift for Daddy. Judith said she would think of something and when she did she'd know it would be right. But now there was nothing but muddle in her head.

When she walked into the yard, Hannah heard baying, shouting voices and the judder of a plank thrown against a wall, and she stopped in her tracks. There was a small crowd down by the pigsty, and figures in khaki shirts, with sweat patches on their backs, moving about on the other side of the wall.

The soldiers were still there.

No, she thought. Not that as well.

The shouting intensified, a fearful bellowing accompanied by the clanging of metal on metal. She couldn't tell where it was coming from. It wasn't the crowd, which stood motionless and silent, their eyes fixed on the pigsty. She shrank back with her hands to her ears. She was about to turn and run when David came hurrying towards her.

"Hannah!" he was calling. "Quick! You're just in time."

A MAN LIKE
LEGION

"They're just taking the planks off the pig-sty," David said, "Come on or you'll miss it." Hannah looked at him and blinked. The idea that she should want to see this seemed peculiar to her. Hurry? To see something so disgusting?

"I don't know..." she started to say, but her head was filled with those strange, warbling shouts and with banging from somewhere.

What was it? Tins tapping, hammering? Why?

"Quick!" said David, and there was so much urgency about him, such excitement in his face, that she allowed him to take her by the sleeve and lead her down to the pig run.

William was there, and Mrs Corbiss, looking fierce with her arms folded, and several others from Ackford. A face turned as David pulled Hannah up to them. Mrs Prothero, who lived next to the Post Office. She leaned close to Mr Prothero and said something in his ear. Then Mr Prothero looked round and, for a second, they were both staring, their faces somehow accusing Hannah. She looked round for Elizabeth but there was no sign of her.

The noise was much louder down here.

"What's all that banging?" she asked.

"They've got soldiers at the back of the pigsty," said David. "To frighten it out."

Major Bartholomew stood apart from the crowd, watching impassively and tapping a short stick against his open hand. Two soldiers had been posted by the gap in the wall with rifles at the ready. Three more were crouched close by the entrance to the pigsty. They had wrenched most of the planks away with crowbars. A broad man with tattoos on thick red forearms advanced on the pigsty and dropped to one knee. William's net was slung over his shoulder like a cloak.

"It's on the move, sir!" he shouted, and scuttled back a little, feet and knees and knuckles, like an ape. Immediately, the noise from the back of the sty ceased, as if the men there were somehow aware of what had happened.

"Barnes, Glanville," said Major Bartholomew quietly, and the soldiers at the gap lifted their rifles to their shoulders and braced themselves.

The man with the tattoos pulled the net slowly from his shoulder. Major Bartholomew stopped tapping his stick. Everything became still, and there was no sound to be heard except for the crying of a gull over the sea, far behind them.

Then a dark shape crawled into the entrance of the pigsty and the little crowd sucked in its breath. In spite of herself, Hannah tried to see, but her view was partly obscured by shoulders and the backs of heads.

"A man," she heard Mr Prothero say to himself. "Arms and legs like a man."

"A man like Legion," said Mrs Corbiss. "With Satan in him."

"Legion?" said Mr Prothero.

"Mark's Gospel, chapter five. You know your Bible, Prothero. The man possessed by evil spirits..."

"Keep still, all of you," said Major Bartholomew in a level voice. "Throw the net in your own time, Baker."

The man nodded without taking his eyes off the creature in the pigsty.

"And stay well to the side in case I give the order to fire. Ready with the irons, the rest of you."

Hannah saw one of the men reach behind him and feel for some chains with stretched fingers. His hand brushed the pile of links. It moved and settled and the links clicked together. A sharp sound, like a door suddenly unlocked. The monster twisted its head in the direction of the noise.

Grey-green flesh tight on a round skull like a seal's. A bare face with a slit of a mouth. No fronds covering it. Two pits of eyes. Two, set like a man's. Beneath them, dark streaks, like water on dust. Those eyes pierced into Hannah's then, so she could hardly take in anything else.

It can't see properly, she thought.

Then it ducked clumsily down as if it intended to withdraw to the shadows. But Baker was standing up in a smooth, unhurried movement. And his red arm was swinging and the net unfurling in the air.

There was shouting and a blur of motion. Boots scrabbling desperately in the straw. The chains snaking and rattling. The net heaving with sudden life. And a howling, croaking noise boomed beneath all the human cries.

A band of iron was snapped shut on the monster's arm. Another on its leg. Green-black fingers pierced the net and ripped it as if it were cotton. Baker pulled hard on one of the chains and the monster tumbled backwards and became still.

"Got it, sir! Got the beggar!"

"Good man, Baker. Hold firm."

Before she turned away, Hannah caught sight of one of the soldiers staggering away from the crush of bodies. He was rubbing frantically at a patch of slime on his tunic, and there was a jagged scratch across his white cheek.

She burst into the kitchen, and the door slammed against the wall and juddered behind her. Elizabeth was sitting in the armchair, staring at the empty fireplace.

"Well?" she said without looking up.

"They've chained it," said Hannah breathlessly.

"Good."

"There were two men with guns and—"

"I don't want to know. They've got it, Hannah, and that's all that matters now."

But that wasn't all that mattered, surely. Somehow, Hannah needed to understand the things she had seen and heard down at the pigsty. She wanted to find the words that would explain it all to her sister; to tell her about the soldier who had been scratched, about the look of fear and disgust on his face, about the booming cry of anguish that came from the monster.

And Elizabeth didn't want to know. She didn't take her eyes from the fireplace, even when the confusion of shouting and the rattle of chains could be heard moving up the track towards them. The sound faded slightly as the soldiers skirted round the side of the cottage, then grew loud again just outside the kitchen window. Hannah walked quickly across the kitchen and looked out. She saw a strange procession climbing the slope up to the sea path.

Major Bartholomew was walking stiffly at the front, swinging his stick like a man on a walk in the country. Behind him the red-armed soldier tugged on a chain over his shoulder. The monster slouched at the end of it, forcing itself along on its knuckles and short back legs. It swung its heavy head from side to side. A second chain dragged on one ankle and was held slackly by the soldier with the scratched face. Then came the men with the rifles and half a dozen others carrying ropes and spare chains.

The people of Ackford followed at a distance. The shouting was coming from them. The iron bands that secured the monster seemed to have released them from their silence. They jeered and hooted, some of them waving their arms in a kind of wild dance and some laughing fiercely. Hannah saw one of Ackford's fishermen dart forward and push his way between two soldiers to spit at the monster's back. Mrs Prothero caught sight of Hannah at the window and stopped. Her mouth was set in a firm line. She stared severely for a moment and then hurried on.

"Come away from there, Hannah," said Elizabeth. "There's nothing more to see."

Hannah turned her back on the procession and the clamour began to die away. She watched Elizabeth stand up wearily and take the tin box from the mantelpiece.

"I promised you something from Daddy's box," she said.

She carried it to the table and opened it, taking out a number of objects and arranging them in a tidy group. A tiny gold locket, a pocket watch on a silver chain, an old leather purse, a medal and some coins, a ring, and a black prayer book. It troubled Hannah to see them, not only because they brought back sharp memories of her father, but because she remembered taking them from the box herself one rainy day.

She'd thought she was alone in the cottage and she'd knelt by the fire, studying each object carefully before lining them up on the rug. The rain had been drumming on the kitchen window and, from time to time, drops spat down the chimney on to the fire.

And that's where Daddy had found her. Suddenly he was standing over her, rain dripping off him and the red light from the fire moving over his wet face. He had gathered the things up and tipped them back into the box. And he had stared at her for a moment without saying a word, before banging the box roughly back on the mantelpiece.

Hannah burned with shame at the memory

of this, as if her cheeks were still hot from the glow of the fire.

Elizabeth pushed the locket to one side with her finger.

"He said I was to have this," she said.

Their mother's picture in a little oval of gold.

"The ring is for Judith, if she wants it, and this is yours."

She picked up the watch and it spun at the end of its silver chain. Hannah opened her hand. The watch was cool and heavy. She closed her hand and pushed it into her pocket.

I wanted to give something to Daddy, she thought, but he's given something to me.

"What's the promise I have to make?" she asked.

"It's easy enough," said Elizabeth. "Nothing you wouldn't want to do anyway. You must be confirmed."

"Confirmed?"

"Yes. You know, confirmed into the church. Daddy would like to think that you were taking your first communion before the end of the summer."

Hannah thought about the rector, his anxious, boyish face, and the way he always ignored her.

"Must it be up at St Peter's?" she asked.

"Of course it must, Han. Where else would you go to be confirmed?"

"I don't know."

"What's the matter, then?"

"Nothing. Only, the rector…"

"What about the rector?"

"I don't like him, Elizabeth. He doesn't take any notice of me and…"

"You don't get confirmed for the rector's sake, girl. It's something you have to do for God, and for Daddy, of course."

"Yes, I suppose so."

"So you promise. For Daddy's sake."

"Of course I will."

Elizabeth began to return the other things to the box.

"Has Judith said anything to you?" she asked.

"No. Why?"

"She has funny ideas, Hannah. You mustn't take any notice of her."

"Must she be confirmed, then?"

"Of course she must."

"But she wouldn't before, would she?"

"No. She wouldn't before."

Two years ago their father had suggested that it was time for Judith to be confirmed, and Judith had refused.

"I can't say all those things if I don't believe them," she had said angrily.

She was pacing up and down outside the back door while Daddy sat on a stool peeling potatoes. Little Hannah knelt at his feet, waiting to take the peelings over to the pigs, and listening to every word.

"It would be wrong," Judith said.

"That's why you have to be instructed, Jude. So you can learn to believe."

He spoke in a calm, imploring voice, working steadily at the potatoes and frowning with concentration.

"I sit in church every week. What more do I have to learn?"

"Elizabeth was confirmed. What's so different about you?"

"Elizabeth is Elizabeth. I can't make promises about things I don't believe."

"You don't believe in God?"

He sounded hurt.

"I don't know," she snapped.

She walked up the path, flouncing her skirt this way and that. Then she stopped at the linen post and put her arms dreamily around it.

"I don't know," she added softly.

"Then tell me where this spud came from if God didn't make it?" Daddy said, suddenly angry.

He held up a potato so that the water dripped down his arm and ran off his elbow in a little stream. He held it so tight that his fist was shaking. Judith laughed.

"You dug it up," she said. "And it was you

who planted it, and you who piled on straw to keep the frost off. And you hated every minute of it. I never saw God out there lending you a hand."

"You mind what you say, Jude."

"And you're supposed to peel it, Daddy, not carve great chunks out of it. If it really is God's spud, you should treat it with more respect."

Hannah flinched as he jumped to his feet. The stool clattered back into the kitchen and the bowl fell off his knees, sloshing water and potatoes on to the path.

"That's enough! That's enough of your back-answering!"

For a second, a look of fear crossed Judith's face. Then she opened her eyes wide and stared back at him. Hannah crawled on to the path and started gathering up the potatoes.

"Leave them be," shouted Daddy, and she shrank back.

He hardly ever shouted at his girls. At the sea and the wind and the earth sometimes, but hardly ever at his girls.

"The pigs can have the lot for all I care," he muttered and stalked off into the kitchen.

The water soaked slowly away and the potatoes stayed where they had dropped for the rest of the afternoon. Eventually Elizabeth came out with a bowl of clean water to collect them up and finish peeling them.

Later that evening they sat round the table

in silence and ate the potatoes with some broad beans and some pieces of bacon. Hannah looked at them on her plate; at the flat ones Daddy had sliced, and the smooth ones peeled by Elizabeth.

It was a while before any of them mentioned potatoes, or God, again. And no one said a word on the subject of confirmation till after Daddy died.

"It'll only take an hour," Elizabeth said. "And it won't be so bad. You'll see."

"Yes," said Judith. "I expect we will."

"It's not for my sake, Jude. It's..."

"I know. It's for Daddy's sake. You've told me enough times. Come on, Hannah."

She swung a shawl over her shoulders and marched out. As they rounded the corner of the cottage, Hannah looked back to give Elizabeth a little wave. Elizabeth unfolded her arms and her frown became a brief smile. She waved back and went indoors. Judith neither looked nor waved.

"You coming with me, Han?" she said as she strode up the track on to the sea path.

"Of course I am," Hannah answered. "We said we'd go together."

"And a promise is a promise, isn't it?"

It occurred to Hannah then that perhaps Judith didn't want her there. Perhaps she wanted to face the rector on her own. To tell him what's what, as Mrs Corbiss would say, out of earshot of a little sister who might carry news of the conversation back to Elizabeth.

"I can wait outside for you, if you like," Hannah said.

"Oh no, Han. That would never do."

"Why not?"

"He might turn out to be a proper Romeo, mightn't he?"

"What, the rector?"

"You never know."

It was true. Of course. Her beautiful sister alone with a young priest. That would never do.

"You keep an eye on him, Hannah. If his ears start turning red, you cough or something. All right?"

Judith laughed and skipped ahead. She took the shawl from her shoulders and held it up to keep the sun off her face.

"Anyway," she called back to Hannah, "I didn't mean that."

"What did you mean, then?"

"Are you coming where I'm going? That's what I meant."

"To the church?"

"I'm not going to the church."

"But Elizabeth said…"

"Elizabeth said that Daddy said that God said… No, Han. I don't need her to tell me what Daddy wanted."

"But he did want us to be confirmed, Jude."

"Maybe. And maybe I will go and see her precious rector one day. Not today, though."

There was still laughter in Judith's face, but when Hannah stopped walking and looked at her with a puzzled expression, she became suddenly serious.

"I do know what Daddy wants," she said. "I dream about him. Not the way he was – at least, not always – but the way he still is. Sometimes it's like he's not really dead, Hannah. Do you know what I mean?"

Hannah wasn't sure that she did know what Judith meant.

"Where are you going," she asked, "if you're not going to the church?"

"To the castle, to see the monster," said Judith, and she laughed again and ran ahead.

JOHN
UNDERWOOD

The soldier tapped on Major Bartholomew's door and bowed his head, listening. There was no reply.

"He gets carried away sometimes," he smiled back at Judith. "Sometimes he don't hear the knock."

He pushed the door open a little but they saw at once that the room was empty. The tin of paints was still on the desk. A few green shrubs had been added to the landscape, but it seemed to Hannah that the Major must have suddenly tired of the work and abandoned it. A brush had been dropped carelessly on the picture, leaving a trail of green smudges over the sky.

"I think I know where he might've gone," said the soldier, shutting the door and leading them back to the large, round room at the centre of the castle.

"Don't worry. We'll find him, miss."

He smiled at Judith again, and Judith smiled back.

Hannah remembered waiting in this room with Mrs Corbiss. She remembered the way the old woman had stood firmly on the little wooden bridge and forced her way into the castle by the strength of her will. Judith had managed it differently, by being sweet and pretty. Two ways to get what you wanted. Hannah wondered which way would work best for her. She didn't have Judith's wide blue eyes, and she didn't have the fierce authority of Mrs Corbiss.

"I've got a feeling he's gone down to the dungeon," the soldier said. "I'll go and see if you like."

"We'll come too, shall we?" said Judith.

"It's not a nice place, miss. A bit mucky and dark. And, well, you know..."

"What?"

"We've put that thing down there. The monster."

"But that's why we've come," said Judith. "We don't mind that at all, do we Hannah?"

Hannah did mind but she shook her head and followed them over to a dark staircase in the corner of the room.

"I thought so," whispered the soldier. "You'll find him down there."

He closed the door behind them and they were plunged in darkness. Hannah heard his boots treading quietly up the spiral staircase. She felt for Judith's arm and clung to it. They were standing on a broad slab at the top of a flight of steps which led down to the dungeon. A thin light filtered in from an opening somewhere in the ceiling. Some way below them there was a yellow glow and she tried to fix her eyes on that. The place smelled of cold, damp sand. After a while she felt herself leaning forward, as if she were about to topple into a pool of blackness. She squeezed Judith's arm harder.

Words floated up out of the darkness.

"It is my duty to ask:"

Major Bartholomew. His voice soft and steady. Echoing slightly.

"You see, I have to write reports and send them up the line to headquarters. They never reply but I have to send them anyway. That's why I have to ask."

The yellow glow began to take shape. An oil-lamp. The Major crouching by it, his back to them, his elbows on his knees.

"I feel rather foolish, of course. And I can't tell whether you can hear and understand but refuse to answer. Or whether what I'm saying makes no sense to you at all. Whether you are, in fact, what they say you are: some wild beast, a dumb creature."

Hannah felt Judith move forward. She heard her foot scratch over the stone step and drop down to the next one. She tapped the space in front of her with her toe, found the edge and dropped awkwardly down, too. Reaching out with her right arm, she met nothing but space. She imagined she was standing an inch away from the sheer side of the steps.

"Have you come from the marshes, for instance?" the voice went on. "Or from the sea? And what have you seen there? Can you answer me? I want to give you the chance to answer if you can. If you tell me nothing ... well, you will leave me with no choice but to..."

And suddenly he stopped talking and stood up. He picked up the oil-lamp and held it close to his face.

"Barnes? Is that you?"

"No," said Judith, her voice light and clear. "We've come from the cottage. My sister was here before..."

He moved quickly to the foot of the steps. The lamp swung in his hand and bars of black and pale grey loomed wildly beneath their feet.

"What are you doing here?" he said sharply. "Come down where I can see you."

They edged their way down and his round face became clear. He was looking at Hannah through the yellow moons of his glasses.

"It's me, Major Bartholomew. Hannah."

"Yes, of course. I can see you now. And this must be Judith."

His voice became soft again.

"Have you been here long?"

"Just a moment or two," said Judith.

"You'll think it strange," he said, laughing a little. "Talking to myself like that. And perhaps it is. I have to find out what this thing can understand, though. It looks remarkably like a man to me and … well, I have to be sure."

But it's a monster, Hannah thought, not a man. And she realized that it was down there with them, lurking in the dark somewhere. A monster in the dark, watching them.

"I needed to see it, Major Bartholomew," said Judith. "I hope that's all right."

"Yes, yes. Of course."

He turned away from them, his shadow lurched off sideways and the darkness closed in again. Judith moved after him and Hannah suddenly found herself alone. She stumbled forward and clutched her sister's shawl.

Then she saw with relief that there was a wall of bars a few paces ahead of them.

"It's in there," said Major Bartholomew.

Judith went slowly to the bars and held on to them. Her shawl slipped from her shoulders and hung in Hannah's hand. Hannah twisted it in her fingers and stared down at it.

She did not want to see the monster ever again.

Elizabeth was waiting for them on the sea path. She watched them walking slowly towards her and her face was white with anger. She did not speak until they drew level with her.

"You said you were going to the church."

"I know what I said but..."

"You lied to me, Judith. And you led Hannah astray."

"How do you know? How do you know where we've been?"

"I don't. But I know where you haven't been. The rector's come to find out where you were."

"He would."

Judith pushed past her and dropped down to the track which led to the cottage.

"You can't go on like this, Judith," Elizabeth called after her. "You know you can't. The rector's waiting in the kitchen and you can see him now. Do you understand?"

His name was John Underwood. The Reverend John Underwood. Someone must have told Hannah that at the funeral but there were things about that day she couldn't remember at all. He sat at the kitchen table with his back to the open door. Clearing his throat and combing his fingers back through his hair, he told them a little about himself. He -paused several times during this, restarting some sentences and letting others trail away to nothing.

"Well ... we don't want to spend all the time talking about me, do we? I mean to say, I just thought ... I just thought..."

He combed his hair again and tried a smile.

"What?" said Judith.

She sat impassively at the other end of the table, fiddling with a stalk of grass. Hannah noticed that she was wearing the ring from Daddy's box on the middle finger of her left hand.

"Well," he said, "I thought we might just ... that we might merely begin with a chat."

"A chat?"

She looked up at him with amused contempt.

"Yes. So we can get to know each other and..."

"I thought we were supposed to get to know God."

"Yes. Yes, we were. I mean, we are. But ... well, we might find it easier if..."

"This isn't my idea, you know," said Judith.

"It's not..."

"We're here because Elizabeth wants us to be. Didn't she tell you it was her idea?"

"No. I mean, she did explain that you'd promised…"

"Good. And I keep my promises, Mr Underwood. So perhaps you'd better carry on."

"Carry on?"

"Chatting."

"I see. Yes."

Judith switched her attention back to the grass. He cleared his throat again and began to ramble on uncomfortably, telling them a little about the church, and a little about God. Hannah watched Judith's fingers and paid scant attention. At one point she sensed that he was staring intently at his own hands and she risked a glance in his direction. She saw him framed in the brightness of the kitchen door, one ear almost red with the light shining through it. She looked at Judith and knew that she had noticed it, too. Judith raised her eyebrows and touched her own ear with the tip of her finger. Hannah snorted and tried to make it sound like a cough. It seemed wrong to laugh when she was so unhappy, but she couldn't help it.

"Are you all right?" John Underwood asked her.

There was concern in his eyes but Hannah could only see the red ear glowing on the side of his head.

"Would you like some water … or…"

"No," choked Hannah. "It's just a tickle."

She tried to think of something else. Something to stop her laughing out loud.

The monster.

Yes. That ugly creature in the dungeon up at the castle. Nothing else seemed funny when she thought about that. And it had crashed through all her thoughts about Daddy.

The rector was talking about God's love for his people. The rector who had prevented William from crushing the monster down on the beach.

He's just weak, thought Hannah. A weak and silly man.

She heard Judith sigh. Then John Underwood stopped in the middle of what he was saying and both girls looked up at him.

"May I ask you a question now?" he said after a pause.

"If you like."

"Thank you. How many times?"

"What?"

"You promised Elizabeth you would attend confirmation classes. How many times did you promise to speak to me?"

Judith frowned uncertainly and didn't answer.

"You don't want to be doing this," he went on. "That's obvious. So have you agreed a limit with your sister?"

"Five," said Judith shortly.

"Five. I see.' He spread his hands on the

table and stood up. "Well, four to go, then."

"What do you mean?"

"That's enough for today. There's not really much point going on, is there?"

He wiped his face with a white handkerchief and walked to the door.

"Unless," he said, turning. "Unless Hannah would like me to continue."

"No," said Hannah. "Thank you very much."

"Then I'll say goodbye. Perhaps I'll see you at the church next week."

He bobbed his head and went out of the door. Judith watched him walk up the path and disappear round the corner of the cottage.

"Who does he think he is?" she asked herself. "Just who does he think he is?"

Then she laughed and took Hannah by the hand.

"Don't look so glum, Han," she said. "Only four to go. And he'll hate the sight of us before he's finished."

And she went upstairs, humming to herself, almost as if she were happy. Hannah closed her eyes. Now that she'd started to think about the monster again, she couldn't stop the thoughts tumbling over themselves in her head.

Elizabeth wants it killed, she thought, and I do, too. But no one is doing anything about it. The soldiers have chained it up and Major

Bartholomew is trying to question it. How can it possibly answer? A repulsive slug with arms and legs.

Later that afternoon she took a slow walk into Ackford. As she climbed the steep slope past the bakery, she glimpsed a figure at the open door of the baker's cottage. The face was in shadow but sunlight fell on one round forearm, folded under a broad bosom. Plump Mrs Rayner, who'd always slipped an extra white roll in the bag when she called for bread.

"We shan't miss one," she used to say in a hushed voice, twirling the bag nimbly so that its corners stood out like little ears. "Only, don't tell your dad."

Hannah smiled and turned to say hello, but Mrs Rayner looked away, as if she hadn't seen her. The door banged to, rattling the brass knocker, and Hannah was left feeling foolish, with the smile still on her face. She remembered Mrs Prothero's hard eyes staring in at the kitchen window.

They blame us for the monster, she thought. For bringing something evil into the heart of Ackford. Yes. It's left its slime on us, just as it did on that soldier, the one it clawed across his cheek.

She went up the steps by the side of The Hat and Feathers and wandered towards the harbour.

So why is it still alive?

For Daddy's sake, and for Judith's sake, it should be killed. We should be clear of it. We should wash down every stone it's dragged itself over. Sluice it clean. Put down fresh grass that smells of meadow and not rotting seaweed.

But it still lives, skulking down there in the dungeon at the heart of the castle.

If I were a man. If only I were a man. Not for always, but just for that.

The thought shocked her. Like a clear note struck from a bell, ringing and ringing in her head. She stopped walking and closed her eyes.

You will know, Judith had told her. You will know when you think of the right thing to do. And surely Judith would understand this. She would understand it perfectly.

To do something for Daddy. Get rid of the monster.

She saw David, painting an upturned boat. He was singing tunelessly to himself as he pulled the brush along the fat curve of the boards. A pale blue line, like a band of sky.

Yes, she thought. David.

She watched him for several minutes before he realized she was there.

"Oh," he said, dropping the brush into its

tin and wiping his hands on his trousers. "I didn't see you there."

"You can carry on if you like," Hannah said.

"Right. I will, then. Dad wants this done before dark."

Hannah sat on the harbour wall and stared down at the water. Beneath the sparkling surface she saw columns of red-brown weed waving and leaning with the tide.

"Did you want anything?" David asked after a while.

"No. Why?"

"Nothing, really. I only thought..."

"I'll go if you like," she said, jumping up.

If people didn't want them, if they thought the Richards girls were contaminated...

"No," said David. "I don't mind, Hannah. Unless you want to go..."

She studied his face for a moment and then sat down again.

"Old Jasper said you been up to the castle," he grinned. "Said he saw you and Jude coming away."

"Did he?"

"Talk to Bartholomew, did you? Been sorting things out?"

"What things?"

"You know. Things."

"The monster?"

"Yes."

"Judith wanted to see it. We went down to the dungeon."

"No."

"They didn't mind. You could go yourself if you wanted."

"I don't know," he said doubtfully. "Maybe I would."

She glanced over her shoulder at him. He had stopped painting and was looking down at her.

"You're not scared, are you?"

"What? No, of course I aren't. I stood guard over the pigsty, didn't I? I might go up there," he added. "You know what old Jasper says? He says that thing might bring us all a bit of luck."

"Luck? After what it did to Judith?"

"I'm only saying what he told me. And anyway, the monster's not natural, is it? It's kind of like magic. If you touch it or something..."

"Touch it?" said Hannah, screwing up her face in disgust.

"I'm only saying. If you touch it, you might get some of that magic for yourself." He nodded at the sky. "It's like all this sun. They say the crops are baking in the ground. If we don't get rain soon, we'll be in for a real bad harvest."

"I don't see what that's got to do with it."

"Well," he said, shrugging and dipping his

brush in the tin, "maybe the monster'll bring a bit of luck, that's all. Maybe it'll make it rain."

"It's been here long enough," Hannah said. "It doesn't look like rain to me."

"No. That's true, I suppose."

She stood up and wandered round to the other side of the boat, touching the wet paint with the tip of her finger.

"They don't all think that, do they?"

"What?"

"That it'll bring luck. Some of them think it's brought a curse."

"A curse?" he said. "Who thinks that?"

"Mrs Corbiss. And there's others…"

"What others?"

"The Protheros. I'm sure they think it's all our fault. Me and Judith and Elizabeth."

"How can it be your fault, Hannah?"

"I don't know. But it hasn't brought much luck, has it?" she said slowly, watching his face as he painted. "Unless…"

"What?"

"Well, maybe it has to be killed first."

"Killed?" he said.

"Maybe the luck will change when it's dead."

"I don't know. The rector says we mustn't."

"The Reverend John Underwood," she laughed bitterly, and saw that David was blushing. "What does the rector know? He's

77

never seen a monster before. He doesn't know what he's talking about."

"I know all that, Hannah, but…"

"Everyone's too scared to go against him, though, aren't they? You and everyone else. There's no one in Ackford with the courage to kill it. But if I was a man, David," she added deliberately, "I know that's what I'd do."

RAW FISH

It was too hot to sleep. Hannah lay on her bed, gazing at the limp curtains and the dusky blue sky beyond. When she closed her eyes she saw David's face peering at her across the hump of the upturned boat, his brows folded in bewilderment. She saw him at the moment when he realized what she really meant.

Someone to kill the monster? Is that what has to be done?

But it was only his look that asked. Neither of them had spoken. And she couldn't detect any answer in his eyes.

She got up, went quietly to the window and looked out at the sea. A wide, milky moon was hanging over a grey expanse of flatness. She could hear its soft breathing, like whispered questioning, and she imagined dark things moving slowly in its depths.

"Judith," she said softly, turning away from

the window. "Are you awake?"

Judith's bed was a jumble of shadows in the corner.

"I've been thinking about what you said. About what I should do. Jude?"

But the shadows had become a tangle of sheets. The bed was empty. She trod carefully downstairs. Standing on the bottom step, she saw Judith moving nimbly about the kitchen. There was a cloth on the table and she was hurrying backwards and forwards, arranging things on it. An apple, some bread and cheese. Hannah watched her go to the pantry and take out a fish on a white plate. Its silver flank shone briefly in the light from the window.

"What are you doing?" Hannah asked.

"Oh, Han," said Judith, holding her hand to her heart. "Why aren't you in bed?"

"I couldn't sleep. What are you doing?"

"Nothing. Just preparing something to eat."

"What, now?"

"No. No, I ... I thought I'd take it out with me tomorrow. Go for a long walk."

"Can I come with you?"

"I'm not sure, Han. We'll see."

And that probably meant no. Hannah decided not to say anything else to Judith just then. She went back upstairs, straightened the sheets and got into bed.

A long walk tomorrow. With a parcel of food. Bread and cheese and raw fish. Why should she take raw fish, though? Where was the sense in that?

Hannah slept late and woke to the sound of voices murmuring in the yard. She went sleepily to the small window on the landing and pushed it open. Major Bartholomew was down there, standing with his foot on the bench outside the kitchen. He swished idly at a clump of mint with his stick. The window swung a square of golden sun on to the path in front of him and he looked up and smiled at Hannah. He touched the stick to the shiny peak of his cap and then quickly bent his head to Mrs Corbiss, who was sitting at the other end of the bench.

"The thing is, Major Bartholomew," Mrs Corbiss was saying, "that creature came out of the sea in the self-same spot where my Corbiss kept his boat. The self-same spot. I shall never forget it. He took the boat out one day and never came back. They found the boat but they never found Corbiss. I thought then there was something evil about it all. And now I know."

"You think you know, Mrs Corbiss," said the Major politely. "You can't be sure. This is some sort of animal. You can't be sure it's evil."

Elizabeth appeared with a mug of tea in her hands. Her dark hair was gathered in a tight bun and Hannah, looking down at her, thought she looked even more grown-up than usual, straight-backed and handsome.

"But it's simple really, Major," said Elizabeth as she handed him the tea. "We don't know what it is – we don't much care – but we do know what it's done."

"Or tried to do. Or, as I say, you think you know."

"We do know, Major, and we want it put to death."

"Yes, well ... I'm afraid I can't do that."

"Why not?" asked Mrs Corbiss.

The Major gave a short laugh and slapped his boot with his stick.

"Well," he said, "if it's human – and we can't be sure it isn't – it can't be put to death without a trial."

"A trial? For a thing like that?" said Elizabeth.

Still talking about the monster. Nothing but talk.

Elizabeth took two or three agitated steps down the path. When she turned round she opened her mouth to speak but caught sight of Hannah and stopped herself.

"Don't hang out of the window like that, Hannah. Major Bartholomew has come to see us."

Hang out of the window like what? thought Hannah.

Mrs Corbiss and Elizabeth had their faces

turned up to her but all she could see of the Major was the brown disc of his cap. He hung his head and flicked his stick at the clump of mint.

"Get yourself properly dressed, girl," said Mrs Corbiss. "Flouncing about at this hour of the day."

Hannah felt her cheeks grow warm. She withdrew and hurried to the bedroom to dress. A minute or two later she skipped into the kitchen. The white cloth was no longer on the table, she noticed, and Judith's shawl had been taken from its peg by the door.

When she got outside, the Major was still talking about the monster, but there was now an edge of irritation in his voice.

"Well, I'm sorry to labour the point," he said, "but if it's not human…"

"Then it won't matter, sir, will it?" cut in Mrs Corbiss. "You can have it put down."

"Of course it'll matter, woman. Of course it will."

"Why?"

"If it's not human, and I call a trial, then I would be bringing the full weight of the law to bear on a fish. And that will matter. To me." He spread his arms in a gesture of hopelessness. "I shall look … well, foolish."

"But, Major, who will know?"

"Someone. Don't you understand? I've had to write this thing down in my reports. I've sent news of it to headquarters."

He sighed and sat down on the bench, removing his cap and balancing it on his knee.

"Look," he said with forced calm, "suppose I say it's a fish and we don't bother with a trial. What happens then? I don't have to remind you of the goings-on in Europe, do I?"

War, thought Hannah. He means war. Why doesn't he ever use the word? Why does he talk about goings-on or troubles?

"So messages come flying back at me from headquarters," he went on. " 'What about this creature you found, Major Bartholomew? This possible spy? What have you done with him?' What do I say to that? 'We had him killed, sir, and sold on the open market at ninepence a pound.' That is not the military way, Mrs Corbiss. Believe me, they're not used to that."

"Then the first thing you must do, Major Bartholomew," said Mrs Corbiss, "is to make up your mind. Is it human or fish?"

"But that's the point. I just don't know."

"It will be easy enough to find out. If you put it to the test."

"Test?"

"Of course. A test of its soul, the sacred gift from God. If it's human it will have a soul, won't it?"

"How can you find out if it's got a soul?" asked Hannah.

84

"By taking it to the church."

"The church?"

"Of course. You take it to the church to see how it behaves. Does it recognize God's house? Does it bow its head or kneel on holy ground?"

The Major slapped his knees and puffed out his cheeks.

"Is it likely to?" he asked.

"It will know if it's in the presence of God, Major. Of course it will."

"Well ... it is, I suppose, one way of deciding."

"Who would deny it, Major? God's decision, not ours."

The Major sat in silent thought for a while and Hannah noticed Mrs Corbiss watching him closely through narrowed eyes. Then he took a deep breath, stood up and put his cap on.

"I don't know," he said. "I don't know. Perhaps I'll have a word with Underwood."

He nodded briefly at them and strode off.

The church, thought Hannah. What good will that do? This upright military man; this wise old woman. All this talk. Fish and souls and distant wars that were nothing to do with Ackford. Just putting off what must be done.

Hannah propped the stiff yard broom against the draining-board and stood a pail in the sink.

She watched the water gush into it and rolled up her sleeves.

"What are you doing?" Elizabeth asked, suddenly behind her.

"Just a bit of scrubbing."

"There's no need. We've cleaned the place twice over since ... over the last week."

Hannah hefted the pail out of the sink.

"I like to keep busy, though," she said.

"I know that, Han, but we can't keep using water like this. We have to be careful..."

"I'll go without water if it runs low. I won't mind."

"You might not mind, but..."

"It's for the pigsty, Elizabeth," Hannah said deliberately. "I have to clean the pigsty out."

And Elizabeth smiled a tight-lipped smile and nodded.

"Well, yes," she said. "Good idea. And maybe we can burn some of the wood and things."

The chickens picked their way into the pig run as Hannah and Elizabeth made a pile of straw and planks in a clear space. Elizabeth shooed them away and put a match to it. Standing side by side, the sisters watched pale yellow flames run along the planks and the straw crackle and blacken.

"It'll burn fast in this heat," said Elizabeth after a while. "I'll fetch some more stuff to feed it."

She went back to the cottage and Hannah set about scrubbing out the pigsty. She pressed down hard on the broom, scratching it over and over the stones, pushing puddles of dark water into every corner. And frowning fiercely as she worked. There wasn't much evidence that anything had been there, nothing that she could be sure of, but she scoured the place as hard as she could.

Then Elizabeth came back and threw something on the fire. It landed with a whump and sent smoke rolling out flat. Hannah looked over her shoulder and saw the collar of a blue jacket flopped against a charred plank. A button at the neck. Years ago she'd sat on Daddy's lap and twiddled that button in her fingers.

Elizabeth was a swirling shape beyond the smoke. She was cradling a bundle of clothes to her chest. Some familiar, creased jumpers, a knitted hat.

"Oh dear," she said to Hannah, rubbing her face with the back of her wrist. "The smoke stings your eyes."

She opened her arms and the bundle dropped on to the fire. For a moment or two the crackling flames were smothered.

"I couldn't bear to see them on anyone else, Han," she said. "I know it's wasteful but…"

Then she turned her back on the fire and

walked quickly away. Hannah watched her go and then pressed on even more ferociously with her sweeping. When she paused to look at the fire again, she hoped she would see nothing else she would recognize. But a wrinkled sleeve had fallen out of the flames, as if it were trying to clutch at something. The sight of it, or the stinging of the smoke, made the back of her throat ache. She took the broom handle and lifted the sleeve gently on to the fire. Her face prickled with the heat, but she was glad of that.

The smoke curled and wafted aside. Someone was leaning on the wall and looking at her. Judith. Her hair fell in wisps across her face and the white cloth was draped over her shoulder.

"Was this Elizabeth's idea?" she asked.

"No. I wanted to clean out the pigsty so…"

"I mean the fire. She had no right to do that, Hannah."

"Don't be angry, Jude. She couldn't give them away, could she?"

"Maybe not," said Judith.

She folded her arms on the wall and rested her chin on them. Hannah threw the broom aside and went to her.

"I've just been thinking," she said.

"Have you?"

"Do you remember when we kept pigs here?"

"Yes, I remember," said Judith, her eyes fixed on the fire.

"The old sow and the little ones running about and squealing?"

"What about it?"

"Just that sometimes Daddy had to slaughter one of them. We didn't like it but it had to be done."

"Yes," said Judith. "There's lots of bad things have to be done sometimes."

"That's true, isn't it, Jude? We loved the little pigs but ... well, if there was something else to be slaughtered now ... and no Daddy to help..."

"We'd have to do it on our own."

"We would, wouldn't we?"

Like the monster, Hannah thought, and she tried to will Judith to understand without having to say the words. If we have to kill the monster ... and Daddy's not here to help us... You see that, don't you? And the monster's not a pretty little pig; it's an unfeeling, cruel brute...

Judith's cheek was resting on the cloth. The cloth she had wrapped the food in, the bread and cheese and the raw fish. Raw fish.

"Where have you been?" Hannah asked suddenly.

"Just for a walk. Why?"

"Where?"

"If you must know, I went up to the castle."

"To the monster."

"Yes. To the monster."

"And you took it food…"

"No one else had thought to feed it. Only scraps, and green water in an old bowl. Poor thing."

Poor thing?

Judith, of all people, taking it food.

"He was so hungry, Han. He didn't touch the bread and things, but he took the fish… It was … disgusting…"

She hesitated and half closed her eyes, as if she could see the thing eating all over again.

"It was disgusting, the way it sucked on that fish. But you couldn't help feeling sorry for it. You had to pity it, Hannah. You did."

Hannah gazed at her, unable to speak. She felt foolish. Why hadn't she seen it before? A raw fish. Of course it was for the monster.

"Daddy wouldn't mind," said Judith, squinting at Hannah from the cradle of her arms.

"What?"

"If there's chickens to kill, it doesn't have to be you who does it. Daddy wouldn't want that, and we could easily ask William…"

She sat on the beach, hugging her knees. The smell of smoke still lingered on her skirt. Above her the sky was clear and endless and it was too hot for the listless sea to do more than lap tamely against the stones.

An hour ago it was easy to think of getting rid of the monster. Now she knew that Judith had taken it food and that confused her. The thought of it being hungry, feeling hunger.

She heard boots crunch over the pebbles and looked up, shielding her eyes from the sun. David was walking towards her along the beach. He nodded a greeting and came to stand beside her. Then he stood for several minutes, with his hands in his pockets, gazing at the horizon. Eventually he cleared his throat.

"Don't say anything to your sisters or my old man," he said tersely. Then looked sideways at her. "But I will help you, Hannah. I'll help you kill that monster."

TELL ME ABOUT YOUR FATHER

"Don't tell me. You've come visiting."

It was Barnes, the soldier who had shown Hannah and Judith down to the dungeons before. He stood at the end of the wooden bridge with one boot wedged on the handrail, blocking the way. Hannah glanced at David, who was leaning casually on his pitchfork and smiling. A remarkably calm smile. She couldn't believe that he was feeling as calm as he looked.

"We just want to see the monster," she said. "We won't be long."

Her heart was beating so hard she thought it made her voice tremble. Barnes, however, didn't appear to notice.

"You're the third lot today," he said, lowering his foot. "I don't know what you all see in the thing. It's not as if it's beautiful."

"Who else has been?" asked David.

"I don't know. People. They just stand there looking. The thing sits in its corner. Nobody moves. Then they go home. It doesn't make sense to me."

He stood aside to allow them off the bridge. Hannah swallowed and started to walk.

And if we get down there, she wondered, what then? Will one strike be enough? And will the monster cry out? Will it howl? And the soldiers. Will they come clattering down to the dungeon? And if they do, what will they find?

She and David hadn't thought enough about all this. They'd hardly talked about it at all. It was too late now, of course. Barnes was ambling towards the castle and they were following him. Slowly. So slowly. Hannah wanted to push by and speed things up but she knew she mustn't do that. They had to appear like the other villagers: casual callers, come to see a freak.

David touched her arm. She looked round at him and saw his forehead dewed with sweat.

"Shall we be left on our own?" he whispered.

"I don't know."

"What'll we do if we aren't?"

It was no good asking that now. They should've planned it properly.

"I'll think of something," said Hannah.

Perhaps she'd pretend to faint and get

Barnes to take her out to the air. It wouldn't be too hard to do that. She was almost overcome by warmth as it was, though her skin felt cold and clammy. As Barnes pushed open the door to the tower and ducked in, a voice came ringing at them from somewhere at their backs.

"Wait there!"

It came from a low, brick building about twenty paces away. A thick-set man with a heavy moustache was leaning his elbows on the bottom half of a stable door.

"Hold up, Barnes," he called.

Then he was striding over the grass, buttoning his tunic as he came. Stripes on his arm. A sergeant. Barnes backed awkwardly out of the tower.

"What's up, Sarge?"

"Where are you off to with this pair?"

He was a huge man, with black eyes under thick brows on a ridge of bone. He glowered at Hannah and David, moving his lips in and out so that the bristles of his moustache brushed against his hooked nose.

"You might guess," said Barnes. "The dungeons."

"And what's this gadget in aid of?"

He wrapped a tanned hand round the pitchfork and pulled it away from David.

"It's a pitchfork," David said lamely.

"I know what it is, sonny. I want to know

why you've brought it up here."

"He came straight from his work," said Hannah. "We didn't think…"

"Leave it against that wall."

"But…"

"But what?"

"Nothing."

"It'll come to no harm," said the sergeant. "So leave it there or clear off now."

The dungeon was less gloomy than it had been when she came with Judith. This time two low-burning oil-lamps were hanging from brackets on the wall, casting a dull golden glow. Hannah glanced once, quickly, in the direction of the bars and saw lumps of darkness and straw piled in a corner. No movement. A crust of bread. An untouched apple.

Barnes seemed content to leave them alone down there. Perhaps he was more nervous of the monster than he pretended to be. And perhaps the stench of something putrid and brackish, part flesh and part vegetation, kept him away.

"It's no good now," hissed David. "Let's go."

"Not yet. We'll have to stay down here a while or they'll wonder why we came."

David shuddered and pulled his shirt out of his trousers to wipe his face. He walked over to the bars and peered in.

"I could barely reach it with the fork, anyway," he said. "It might not've been any good."

"Can you bring a knife?" asked Hannah.

"What? Come again, you mean?"

"You want to give it up, then?"

"No. No, of course not."

"Then can you get a knife?"

"Yes, but a knife won't reach."

"We'll have to get it to come to the bars. Bring a fish, too. It eats fish."

"How can you know what it eats?"

"It does. I know."

Hannah forced herself to join him at the bars. She'd have to do that if David was going to be free to use the knife. It would be no use at all if she cowered out of the way. She'd have to overcome her disgust. She tried to picture it: how she would push the fish through the bars, just as Judith must have done, and how David ... David would...

"We can't come tomorrow," she said. "It'll be too soon. We must wait a day. And see if we can come when someone else is on duty. Barnes might remember us."

"Suppose it's that sergeant. We'd never get past him."

"We've got to get in again. And get this finished with. Things won't be right till we have."

* * *

96

Their second meeting with John Underwood was up at St Peter's, in the vestry. He handed them prayer books and started to talk in that clipped, broken way of his, avoiding their eyes. Hannah said nothing, hardly paid attention. It wasn't that she had no interest in what he was saying; she was content to accept most of it without question. After all, God was God and John Underwood was his priest. She couldn't argue with that. But it was hard to stop thinking about the day after tomorrow. Getting back into the castle without being seen by Barnes or the sergeant. Luring the monster to the bars. And David, with his knife...

Judith was also silent for most of the time. She thumbed through the prayer book, looking at the psalms, taking no apparent notice of what she was being told, answering questions as briefly as she could.

"I really don't know," she said. Meaning "I really don't care".

John Underwood struggled on for a while. Then he stopped and sighed, and said, "Tell me about your father, then."

"What?" said Judith, surprised.

"Your father. I didn't really know him..."

Thoughts of the monster went out of Hannah's head and she became alert. She looked at Judith and saw a spark of defiance in her eyes. Judith snapped her prayer book shut and sat up straight.

"You tell me about yours," she said.

"Mine?"

"Your Father in Heaven. Or Jesus His Son. I don't mind which. Jesus is Father and Son, isn't He?"

"That's what I have been doing," John Underwood said. "But you haven't really shown much interest."

"No, you haven't. You've been giving us rules and regulations. Why don't you tell us about your Father? What he's like?"

"You'd rather hear me talk than tell me about your father, would you?"

"I don't want to speak about him."

"Because he's dead?"

"No. And anyway, he isn't to me. I can still hear him and still see him..."

"As I can."

"What?"

"My Father."

"In Heaven? You see Him?"

The rector smiled down at his knotted fingers.

"Yes," he said. "Well, no. Not exactly."

"How, then?"

"I mean, I am aware of his presence. Which I suppose is what you mean."

"No. I know my father is still with me."

"Tell me, then."

"No."

"All right," he said.

He made a little gesture of resignation and reached across the table to gather in the prayer books.

"He was a fisherman," Judith said quickly.

"Yes?"

"Like yours. But sometimes he worked the plot of land behind our cottage. Between the pigsty and the back yard. Some days I watched him from the kitchen window. Watched him work away and then stop and rest, hating it, then carry on. Because he had to. To try to feed us. And then he died."

She paused and looked slowly at him. Hannah held her breath and waited. For the first time she noticed an old clock ticking somewhere in the room. A short while ago the rector hadn't been able to look at Judith, but now he returned her gaze steadily. And waited.

"And then he died," Judith said again. "Daddy was a fisherman and you buried him in the earth. He belonged to the sea. That was real to him."

"Do you blame me for giving him a Christian burial?" asked John Underwood.

"No..."

"But you behave as if you think it's all my fault. Mine or God's."

"Well," said Judith, lowering her eyes, "God took him away. You said that yourself in the service."

"Yes, and I don't understand why, but…"

He broke off, turning round sharply at the sudden click of a latch and the creaking of hinges. A beam of straight sunlight cut between Judith and John Underwood, and Major Bartholomew leant into the vestry. He squinted and then caught sight of the rector.

"Ah," he said. "I thought I might find you in here."

"Major Bartholomew. What can I do for you?"

"A brief word, if I may, John," said the Major, looming into the room with a smile.

He looked vaguely around at Hannah and Judith, and tapped his hat with his stick.

"Oh. You're busy. I'm sorry. I didn't mean to interrupt."

Judith sighed and stood up.

"Shall we leave?" she asked the rector briefly.

"No need," said Major Bartholomew. "It's only a brief word, as I said. It is Judith, isn't it?"

"Yes."

"Of course. It was rather dark the last time we met. Are you quite well? After your … ordeal?"

"Quite well, thank you."

"And Hannah. I believe you've been to the castle again. I hope you were able—"

"What did you want, Major?" asked John Underwood.

His voice was clipped again, as if the interruption had annoyed him.

"About that business I mentioned last night."

"The monster?"

"The monster, indeed. The fish-human, human-fish, whatever you want to call it. I just wanted to confirm the arrangements for bringing it here."

"Well," said the rector, "I have agreed, I know, but I'm not entirely happy about the idea."

"It's only a test, John. We can't really proceed until…"

"Yes, Major. It's a test. And that is the point."

"Is it?" asked Major Bartholomew, easing himself into a chair.

Judith remained standing. She was looking straight ahead, her eyes glistening, and Hannah guessed that her mind was still fixed on what she had been trying to say to the rector. Hannah hunched her shoulders and sat still. She felt uncomfortable in the presence of the priest and the soldier. The two most important men in Ackford. Talking so earnestly about what had to be done. Talking, talking. If only they knew what she and David planned to do.

"When it comes down to it," John Underwood went on, "you'll be testing God as much as you're testing the monster."

"Will we? I don't see…"

"You're saying God will decide what this thing is. Like some pagan oracle. God is not like that."

"No?"

"Of course not."

"Well, I'm a military man. You mustn't expect me to understand the mind of the Church."

The Major raised his eyebrows conspiratorially at Hannah and winked. These clergymen, he seemed to be saying. Don't they have such funny ideas?

"Tests are no proof of faith," said the rector. "The opposite, in fact. You make it sound as if God is lurking behind the curtain…"

"Yes…"

"…as if he's going to come out and tell us if we've got it right or wrong…"

"That is how I see things rather, yes. A bit like sending reports to headquarters."

"But it isn't like that."

Major Bartholomew breathed deeply and took his stick in both hands. He stared hard at it, flexing it a little before he spoke again.

"You do realize that something must be done about this creature, don't you, John?" he said quietly.

"Of course, but…"

"Human or fish. I need to know which. I don't mind how I find out but I need to know. So…" He paused for a moment and then rose impressively to his feet. "I'm sorry you're not happy but I intend to bring it up to the church. Tomorrow morning, just after nine. Good-day to you."

Hannah watched the diagonal strap of shiny leather across his stiff back as he walked out.

Tomorrow morning. Tomorrow morning the monster would be in the church, with Major Bartholomew and half Ackford peering at it.

How could she do what she planned to do then?

CHANGED BY THE NIGHT

Moonlight from the landing window lit the stairs where Hannah stood. Bars of silver on the treads. All was quiet above. Below was a well of darkness.

I could go back now, she thought. Back to sleep till morning. After all, they'll take the monster to the church tomorrow and prove whatever they have to prove. And maybe then someone will see that it's put to death, and all this will have been for nothing.

As she stood there, something slid over the back of her hand. It was cold and metallic but its touch was as light as a snake's. She didn't recoil because she knew what it was: Daddy's watch chain.

For Daddy's sake, she thought. That's why I can't wait till tomorrow. I must do this for Daddy. Now.

She stepped into the dark and paused. A line

of round chair backs above the surface of the table gradually took shape. Then the edge of the dresser. She began to walk, slowly, but the darkness still felt thick.

She stopped and narrowed her eyes, trying to make out the pattern of flowers on the low armchair by the fireplace, but the pattern would not come.

Instead she saw two pale hands.

Elizabeth was sitting there, her head back, looking at her.

And this time Hannah did recoil. Her heel struck the sewing basket, making it scratch noisily over the floor. Elizabeth's head rolled a little to one side and was still. She wasn't looking at Hannah at all. She had fallen asleep by the empty fire, the stark white pages of a book open on her lap. There was a wisp of hair against her forehead and her lips were slightly parted. She looked so much younger than she did when she was awake.

Hannah took a deep breath and walked on.

Outside, the night air was cool against her face. The moon cast thick shadows into the yard and she had to feel her way to the corner of the cottage. Then things became clear and silver-sharp and she could hurry. Up the track to the sea path.

She saw the figure on the beach at once. Still and solid as a headstone. Waiting where he'd said he'd be. She dropped from the path and ran down the slope of stones. They growled beneath her feet but the figure kept looking out to sea.

"David," she hissed, but as soon as she did so she realized it wasn't him.

Nothing was what it should have been tonight.

This figure was stockier than David and draped in a shawl. It turned slowly and Hannah saw that it was Mrs Corbiss. Her face was in shadow but Hannah could feel the piercing of her eyes.

"The self-same spot," the old woman said in a voice as ancient as the sea. "Where my Corbiss kept his boat."

She rocked slightly, as if her feet were rooted on the beach and she was trying to free herself. Then she came towards Hannah and looked her full in the face. Damp trails of tears ran down her hollow cheeks, following the lines of grainy wrinkles. She showed no surprise that Hannah should be on the beach in the small hours of the morning.

"Something evil took him," the old woman said softly, "and something evil has come to Ackford again."

Hannah said nothing.

She'll ask me why I'm here, she thought, and I won't know what to say.

But Mrs Corbiss sighed and walked straight by her, moving slowly on, up the shingle towards her cottage. Hannah watched her stooped back disappear in the dark. Then she heard the grate of stones again, and David emerged from the shadows of a bush on the sea path and ran on to the beach.

"She saw you," he hissed.

"I don't think she knew who I was," said Hannah. "It was like she was asleep."

"She'll tell."

"I don't know."

They stood in silence for a moment. She heard the breathing of the massive sea behind her, saw the bright, heavy moon above. She almost sensed the slow turning of the earth. Sensed things moving, changing. She thought of Elizabeth, asleep when she'd seemed to be awake, and of Mrs Corbiss, walking on the beach, and talking to her, but somehow still asleep. Both of them softened by the darkness and strangely changed.

And there will be other changes tonight, she thought. There must be other changes.

"You think we should give this up, Hannah?" said David.

"What?"

"If she tells them…"

"No. I don't care if she does. We have to do it."

"All right," he said. "Let's get it over and done with, then."

* * *

They remained under the shadowy umbrella of a may tree, watching the comings and goings in the castle yard. Everything looked blue or grey. Pale blue where the moon struck, obscure patches of grey elsewhere. There was one soldier at the wooden bridge but they couldn't tell who he was. From time to time he straightened and stretched, then ambled on to the bridge and off again. The darkness seemed to magnify the sound of his boots on the planks.

"Should we go round the back?" David whispered. "Try to get through the wire in the ditch?"

"It won't be easy," said Hannah.

"No, but we can't get in this way…"

She touched his arm and held her finger to her lips.

"Look."

Two men had emerged from the hut and were crossing the yard. They swung belts and fastened them as they went. One of them called to the man at the bridge.

"You'd better come with us."

"What about the bridge?"

"Albert'll take the bridge in a minute. You're needed down below."

The three of them went in at the door in the tower.

"Now," said Hannah.

She stooped and ran without waiting to see

if David would follow, but when she got to the bridge she heard his feet clattering on the planks behind her. The sharp shadows of the bridge struts flickered over them as they scuttled across. They reached the darkness of the castle wall. Hannah pressed her back against the stone with relief and tried to control the heaving of her breath. She could hear David gasping and wheezing beside her.

"I dropped the fish, Han," he said.

"What?"

"The fish. It slipped out of my belt…"

"Why didn't you hold on to it?"

"I didn't know I was going to drop it. I got the knife to carry, too, you know."

"Where is it?"

"Just there."

The fish lay in a circle of dust, halfway between them and the bridge, bright as tin. Hannah saw, as clear as anything, its little pouting mouth and its flat button eye.

"We have to get it," she said.

David took a breath and she sensed him gather himself for a lunge back into the moonlight.

"Wait," she said. "I'll go."

"I dropped it…"

"But I'm dressed darker. I'll go."

But before she could move, they heard a dull thud in the air above them. Then a clank of chains and the click of a latch. A thin strip of yellow-orange light cut into the wall and a window appeared out of nothing. Someone had moved into a room in the castle, about six or seven feet above their heads. There were mumbling voices and, muddled in with them, a low-groaning sound.

"It's the monster," whispered David. "They've moved it."

Hannah made a fist and hit angrily at the castle wall. Why was everything conspiring to frustrate them?

"Can you climb up to the window?" she asked.

"There's soldiers in there..."

"When they've gone," she snapped. "Can you get up there when they've gone?"

"If I stand on your shoulders I might."

"Then we'll wait here till they've gone."

They waited but the soldiers showed no sign of leaving the monster alone in the room. Their voices drifted down to where Hannah and David crouched at the base of the wall.

"Pull on that. Tighten it, man..."

"I am, I am."

"Right. Now go down and fetch the bucket."

"What bucket?"

"What bucket! What do you think? Sling it on that pole, and be careful. I don't want hot coals rolling all over the place."

Hot coals. A bucket of hot coals.

110

Hannah looked questioningly into David's face. His eyes were round and his jaw was trembling.

"What are they doing, Han?" he said.

The light at the window faded and grew strong again as bodies moved about inside the room. A door banged, someone cursed softly, and Hannah heard the sound of something metal being dragged over the floor.

A moment of intense silence.

Then a fierce howl.

David blinked and grabbed hold of Hannah's arm. The sound came again.

Pain. Seering pain. And confusion.

A ragged animal cry, ripping the air and turning Hannah's heart to ice.

"They're hurting it," she said. "Oh God, they're hurting it."

Her hands were clasped to her ears but she couldn't stop the sound. It pierced into her head like a needle. She stumbled to her feet, staggered away from the wall and began to run.

TO THE CHURCH

The cart was pulled by a Suffolk punch borrowed from one of the farmers. Its heavy feet scuffed up dust. The great brown curve of its neck and the swelling of its rump shone softly as it rocked along the lanes to Ackford. Left and right the cart was flanked by two lines of soldiers with rifles. Major Bartholomew walked in front of them, stiff-backed, looking straight ahead.

Most of Ackford had gathered to see the procession go by. They talked in low voices till the cart drew level; then a hush settled on them so that it seemed as if the horse dragged silence along with it.

They saw nothing of the monster itself. It was motionless on the floor of the cart, covered by a tarpaulin criss-crossed with ropes and chains. But they stared as if they could see through cart and tarpaulin, straight to the evil in its heart. And in the silence of their watching there was loathing, and a kind of dread.

Hannah waited in the church porch with her sisters and Mrs Corbiss. She had said very little to anyone all morning, afraid that words might betray the confusion she was feeling. It was like two rivers running through her, she thought. A river of hatred for the monster – a desire to see it dead – and a river of terrible pity at the cry of pain she'd heard. Now the two rivers were running into one, and she was being swept along by it.

She sighed and looked around the little porch. Elizabeth was talking quietly to Mrs Corbiss, their heads bowed towards each other. Daylight had returned them to their former state, and they had that old look of unyielding duty about them.

"It's like a wedding," Judith said, close to Hannah's ear. "All this waiting. It makes you think there should be flowers and things."

They seemed to sense that the monster was coming, even before the procession appeared at the church gate. They stopped talking and looked down the path. The cart moved in a slow half-circle and pulled up. The horse clomped one hoof on the grass and lowered its head.

"At last," whispered Judith. "The groom has arrived."

"Yes," said Hannah dully.

"This is all so silly, Hannah. Bringing the poor thing to the church. What do they think he's going to do?"

Three or four soldiers ran to the back of the cart to lower the tail-gate. They hauled the tarpaulin out and it thudded to the ground. Out of the corner of her eye Hannah saw Judith wince and squeeze her hands together.

Major Bartholomew came briskly up the path towards them.

"It's not moving, Jude," said Hannah. "Do you think it's dead?"

"No. Why should he be dead?"

Hannah didn't answer. The harrowing cry she'd heard at the castle was ringing inside her head again.

"Why should he be dead, Han?" Judith repeated.

"I don't know. It just seems so still."

"They wouldn't bring him here if he was dead, would they?"

"I suppose not."

The Major swept past them into the porch and rapped on the church door with his stick. Hannah was sure that he had seen her, but there were no smiles from him this morning. One of the double doors opened almost at once and John Underwood was standing there, a square black shape against the gloom of the church. Hannah realized that he must have been waiting just inside the door.

"As you see," said Major Bartholomew, half turning back to indicate the soldiers and a following crowd at the bottom of the path, "we have arrived."

"This is not to be a freak show, Major," John Underwood said in a level voice. "I would appreciate it if you kept people away as much as possible."

"Of course."

Major Bartholomew went back to the cart to issue his orders. But none of the Ackford people showed any inclination to come beyond the church gate. Three soldiers took hold of the tarpaulin and began to drag it up the path.

A dead weight, thought Hannah. Like a sack of swedes.

"You won't keep us out of the house of God, will you, Mr Underwood?" Judith asked.

"What?" he said, looking at her sharply.

"It was us he visited out of the sea."

He hesitated a moment and then gestured them in without a word.

They filed in, Hannah and Judith, and then Elizabeth and Mrs Corbiss, bowing their heads as they entered, although the church door was tall and there was no need. It was cool inside the church. John Underwood bent to slide back a bolt. A ripple of echoes ran back through the church. He pushed both doors back to their full extent, then moved to stand in the angle of sunlight he'd let in. Major Bartholomew removed his cap and tucked it under his arm. He looked at the rector, waiting for him to stand aside.

"Please," said John Underwood. "Your men…"

"My men?"

"They have rifles."

"Of course they have rifles. Surely you don't expect…"

"I don't expect them to bring their rifles in here."

"But…"

"Look at it, Major. What harm can it do in that state?"

The Major glanced over his shoulder at the soldiers with their bundle.

"Very well," he said shortly.

One by one the soldiers unslung their rifles and leaned them against the trunk of a gnarled yew. The rector took a step or two backwards and allowed them to drag their burden into the church. One was the hook-nosed sergeant Hannah had seen at the castle.

"Where to now?" asked the sergeant, aiming his question somewhere between the Major and the rector.

"Mr Underwood?" said Major Bartholomew with a deferential nod.

"Down the central aisle," John Underwood said. "Up to the altar steps."

The men shuffled sideways between the carved pew ends, pulling the tarpaulin awkwardly down the aisle. Major Bartholomew and the rector fell in behind them. Mrs Corbiss and the girls remained at the back of the church, watching intently. Mrs Corbiss made the sign of the cross as the soldiers passed her. Their boots clacked and echoed, and the tarpaulin hissed over the marble floor. They came to the altar steps and stopped. They let go of the tarpaulin and stood back. The sergeant went down on one knee and undid thick knots of rope. As he stood again, the tarpaulin fell open and one of the monster's arms flopped out. For a while no one moved.

"Is the creature secured?" asked the Major.

"Yes, sir," said the sergeant. "We fixed a rope on its leg."

"Then take hold of that rope, Sergeant, and hold it firm."

"Sir."

"I can't see properly from here," said Judith, and she moved towards one of the side aisles.

"You should watch that girl," Mrs Corbiss told Elizabeth with a shake of her head. "She isn't right yet and I think she needs watching."

"Judith. Wait," Elizabeth whispered harshly.

But Judith carried on. And Hannah, with one glance back at Elizabeth, followed her.

They paused at the end of the side aisle and,

117

between the backs of two soldiers, they saw the limp arm of the monster and the rounded bone of its shoulder.

"Oh," said Judith. "What's happened to him?"

"Keep your distance, Miss, please," said Major Bartholomew.

"But can't you see? His arm. Those marks."

Black stripes, sticky and glistening.

The monster lay in a pool of dim colours, blues and deep reds, from the stained-glass above the altar. Sad-faced saints looked down on it from tall windows, their hands lifted in gentle and elegant gestures.

"What is it?" Judith asked, looking directly at Major Bartholomew.

His jaw flexed but he did not speak.

"They've burned him," Hannah whispered.

Burned him. Him.

Judith shook her head.

"No," she said. "They can't have…"

"Yes," said Hannah. "I know they have."

The Major shuffled his feet a little.

"We had to do that, Miss Richards."

"Why?"

"A matter of procedure. To see if it would talk."

"Torture, you mean?" said John Underwood quietly.

"Of course not. Interrogation. There are procedures which we have to follow. Don't think I wanted it, man. I had no choice. If it's a man and if it can talk…"

"If it's a man, Major Bartholomew? If it's a man you have to burn its flesh?"

"No doubt it's simple enough to you, Mr Underwood," said Major Bartholomew with exaggerated patience. "But I have other considerations pressing on me. We watch the coast for signs of invasion. You know full well we do. I cannot – cannot – leave things undone when all our lives might be in danger."

He had raised his voice and the echoes dispersed to the corners of the church.

"Don't blame me for what had to be done," he added. "For all our sakes."

"You didn't say you were going to … interrogate it."

"I was not obliged to say, Mr Underwood…"

He said no more because at that point the monster moved. It bent its arm and rolled over on its back. One of the soldiers backed noisily into the lectern. He looked round at the Major, wide-eyed with fear.

"Hold still," breathed the sergeant.

Hannah saw the monster's eyes closed in moist sockets, its mouth gaping and dark. There were teeth, long and brown and curved. They reminded Hannah of the mottled comb Elizabeth used to fix her hair. It made no sound.

Major Bartholomew, his gaze fixed on the

monster, lowered his voice.

"May I remind you why we're here?" he said. "We're here to see what this thing knows of God." He turned to the men. "Allow it some slack, Sergeant."

"Sir."

The hook-nosed sergeant paid out a little rope and immediately the monster curled up like a sleeping cat. For some seconds it remained still. Then it writhed and began to crawl. Its back humped upwards and it lurched towards the soldier at the lectern.

"Step aside," said Major Bartholomew. "Let it go where it wants."

But the soldier, with a tiny whimpering sound, had already stepped aside. The monster clawed at the base of the lectern and began to haul itself up on crooked legs. The lectern was an eagle with a fierce head and broad wings which supported an open Bible. The monster tried to hook on to the Bible to steady itself. Its claw pricked into a white page which folded and crinkled under its touch. Then it twisted its head round and its open eyes, black and wet, saw the people standing round.

Hannah heard a steady voice from the back of the church.

"It does not bow its head."

Mrs Corbiss.

The monster jerked at the sound and the Bible toppled from its stand. It pulled up sharply on its brass chain and the lectern rocked. The monster was standing free, swaying slightly from side to side. Then it fell, barging into the lectern and smashing it down so that an echoing explosion of metal on stone and flapping pages rang up to the roof.

"What more do you need to see?" said Mrs Corbiss. "The creature knows nothing of God, nor can it show him any respect."

"It is in pain," protested John Underwood.

"No," said the Major. "Mrs Corbiss is right. We've seen enough. Sergeant."

Bunching his fists round the rope, the sergeant pulled and the monster's leg was yanked out straight. Hannah winced as if its pain were hers.

"Take up the sheet," he said, and the soldiers hurried forward.

"Wait," cried Judith. "Don't treat him like that."

"Please, Miss Richards," Major Bartholomew began.

"No. What are you doing? What are you going to do?"

"We've found out what we needed to know."

The monster's slow movements were now smothered by the tarpaulin, and the soldiers were working fast at the ropes. Judith turned her frightened face to Hannah.

"What are they doing, Han?"

The Major walked quickly over to them and took hold of Judith's arm.

"For pity's sake, Judith," he whispered. "You of all people shouldn't make a fuss. This thing came out of the sea and nearly took your life away."

"Of course it didn't..."

"We've held off long enough."

"No," Hannah heard herself whisper.

"Yes," Major Bartholomew snapped at her. Then back at Judith, "So let us do what has to be done, and do it quickly, and then get back to the way we were."

Judith was shaking her head. Her yellow hair thrashed the air and she was sobbing.

"And what is it that has to be done?" John Underwood said.

"You know, Mr Underwood," said Major Bartholomew through his teeth.

He turned to the rector, suddenly pushing Judith back into Hannah's arms.

"There'll be no killing in my church," Mr Underwood said quietly.

"Of course there won't. Don't be so simple-minded."

"And neither will the creature leave."

"What?"

"Let it stay it where it is."

"Have you gone mad?"

The rector stepped into the huddle of soldiers kneeling on the edges of the tarpaulin.

Hannah held her breath. Saw them stop what they were doing and look up at him with puzzled faces.

"The creature is still inside the church," he said calmly to them, "and no harm can come to it while it's here. Let go of the rope."

The sergeant blinked at Major Bartholomew and then meekly let the rope slip to the floor. John Underwood took it up.

"I claim sanctuary for the creature," he said.

"You can't."

"I can, Major. You have your procedures, I have mine. The creature stays, and while it stays no harm will come to it."

A CONGREGATION
OF ONE

'Not one monster," said Mrs Corbiss, sweeping furiously down the path to the church gate.

Elizabeth hurried behind her. She seemed anxious to keep up with the old woman.

"Two monsters have come to Ackford," went on Mrs Corbiss. "That man has no right to call himself God's servant. He is infected by evil. He is a monster himself."

The small crowd of Ackford people who had gathered at the gate could see that something was wrong. The church door had swung open and Major Bartholomew and the soldiers had emerged, looking grim and determined. They snatched up their rifles and crunched over the gravel to join their companions at the cart.

"What is it, Major?" William called. "Where's the creature?"

The Major did not answer him. He grabbed the halter and swung the horse's head round. People had to dance out of the way of the turning cart. Then the soldiers were falling into line and marching away. A few orders barked by the sergeant. Not a word to the crowd.

It was Mrs Corbiss who told them what they wanted to know. She stood between the gate-posts, with Elizabeth pale and anxious at her back, and waited rigidly till they were quiet and every face had turned in her direction.

"The creature's still inside," she said, her voice shaking slightly with suppressed rage. "Go to church on Sunday and you'll see it there."

"Dead?" asked William.

"Dead? No! It's crawling on the floor of God's house. Ackford's church. Our church – taken from us and given into the hands of the beast."

The crowd began to murmur questions to itself till the old lady held up both arms stiff in the air to silence them again.

"The rector of St Peter's has granted it sanctuary!"

"No!"

"Yes! It lives and it lives in our very midst, thanks to that boy in there."

"But did it acknowledge God?" someone

called out. "Is that why the rector's keeping it?"

"Did it acknowledge God? I'll tell you what it did."

She paused, looked from face to face, and then lowered her voice.

"It threw the Bible to the ground."

The people caught their breath in shock.

"It ripped pages from the Holy Book," said Mrs Corbiss, "and it threw it to the ground, lectern and all. And for that the rector says it must be saved."

"He can't do that!"

"He has done it. And the Major's gone away because he can't think what to do. That upright military man. Well, *he* may not know, but let me tell you this: God is not mocked. God will not be mocked and for his sake *I* know what I must do."

Another pause. They all waited to see what Mrs Corbiss intended.

"I will set myself at this church door and there I'll stay while that evil thing remains inside. Those of you who love God and know your duty can join me if you like."

"It might be a long wait," William said doubtfully.

"Then a long wait I shall have. But I don't think so. It's halfway dead already."

"And if it doesn't die? If it comes out again?"

"If it comes out, William," said Mrs Corbiss severely, "we'll know what we must do, won't we?"

Hannah stumbled into the sunlight and saw Mrs Corbiss waving her arms and shouting down at the gate. She stood for a moment, not sure what to do. Then she turned and caught sight of Judith in the porch, her cheeks white and her eyes staring, her hand against the church door to steady herself. Hannah ran to her and slipped her arm round her waist.

"You're all right, Jude," she said. "You come with me."

She led her to the shade of the yew tree and they sat down together.

"You shouldn't have come," Hannah told her. "You're not properly well yet."

Judith looked hard at the ground, as if she hadn't heard.

"What have they done?" she said softly. "What have they done to him?"

"I ... I don't know."

Judith looked up at her and blinked.

"You said they burned him, Hannah."

"Yes..."

"You said you knew. Do you?"

"Maybe."

"Do you?"

"I went up to the castle, Jude," she said slowly.

"When?"

"Last night. I heard the soldiers doing things in one of the rooms, and I heard him scream."

"Oh, Han, why didn't you say?"

"I don't know. I was frightened…"

And she was frightened now, frightened and ashamed.

Don't ask me why I went, she thought. Please don't ask.

"They want to kill that poor creature," Judith said. "If it wasn't for the rector he might be dead by now."

"Yes."

"But why? I don't understand. What's he done?"

"They think he was going to kill you. You know that."

"But all this about him being evil…"

"He's a monster, Jude."

"Don't be so stupid. He's a creature from the sea. That's all. You don't think he's anything to be frightened of, do you, Hannah?"

"He's … he's not like any other creature I've ever seen, though…"

"All I know," said Judith with quiet determination, "is that he came the day we buried Daddy. Just as if he heard me calling him."

Hannah looked at her and didn't know what else to say. She glanced back at the crowd by the gate. Mrs Corbiss was still standing before them, one arm lifted in exhortation, like a wayside preacher. She would have known what to say. She would have been very sure. Hannah recalled the way she'd rebuked Elizabeth for letting her sister run down the aisle.

"You should watch that girl. She isn't right yet and I think she needs watching."

Not in her right mind. Touched by evil.

"Come away now," Hannah said at last.

She took Judith's hands in hers, as gently as she could.

"Come home, Jude, and rest."

Hannah came out of the bedroom with the jug of milk she'd taken up to Judith. She moved carefully because the milk was still up to the brim of the jug. By the time she'd brought it from the pantry and taken it upstairs, Judith had fallen asleep. Hannah was relieved, really. It seemed to her that things were a little easier when Judith was asleep. As she steadied herself at the top of the stairs, she looked out of the landing window and saw David down by the pigsty. He was poking about in the blackened sticks of the fire.

She sighed because she knew he'd come to see her and she didn't want to speak to him. Slowly she carried the jug downstairs.

"Did she want it?" asked Elizabeth.

"No. She's already asleep."

"Good. That's for the best."

129

Hannah set the jug on the table and walked to the door.

"Where are you going?"

"Just outside."

"You won't go far, will you?"

"No, I won't go far."

He was crouched over the remains of the fire and so busy with it that he didn't notice her approach. She watched him for a while and then cleared her throat. He looked over his shoulder.

"Oh," he said. "It's you."

"It's me you wanted to see, isn't it?"

"I was just wondering: do they know you went out last night?"

"No. Mrs Corbiss hasn't said anything. What about you?"

"Dad was awake when I got back. I told him. I didn't mean to, but I couldn't help it, Han. It was weird what we seen up there."

"What did he say?"

"I thought he'd fly off the handle but he didn't. Just looked at me sort of funny and nodded."

"He wants the monster dead, too."

"We all do."

"Yes," she said hopelessly. "We all do."

"I didn't say anything about you, though. He thinks it was just me. It's not the same for a girl, is it?"

He smiled shyly, pleased with what he'd

done for her, and she was suddenly irritated by him. Playing with the dead fire like that; where Daddy's old clothes had been.

"Do you have to fiddle around with the fire?" she said. "It's not yours, is it?"

He shook his head and stood up, throwing a charred stick into the nettles by the wall. He wiped his hands on his thighs and was careful not to look at her.

"I don't want to go in the church, Hannah," he said. "The castle's different but I won't go into no church."

"I'm not asking you to."

"That's all right, then."

He took a deep breath.

"Mind you," he said, "no one else'll go there either. Dad says the rector's now cut his congregation right down to one. He says he must be mad to do what he done."

A congregation of one, thought Hannah. And Ackford divided. John Underwood and the monster on one side, everyone else on the other. Of course, there was Judith, too. She was on her own. And Hannah herself. Hannah didn't know where she was.

"Anyway," she said, almost as if it didn't matter, "the monster's nearly dead. It's not going to last very long."

"How'd you know that?"

"I saw it. It can't stand properly. And it shakes."

He thought about this for a moment, and then looked directly at her.

"The sooner the better. That's what I say."

"Yes," she said, then added quickly, "I think so."

Judith woke again in the early evening, as the heat began to seep out of the day. Hannah was scrubbing sheets at the sink when she heard her treading softly downstairs.

"How are you now?" Hannah asked, wiping her arms on the towel.

Judith came blinking through to the kitchen area, lifted the muslin from the block of cheese on the draining-board and cut herself a piece.

"Where's Elizabeth?" she said.

"Outside."

They moved to the door and looked out. Elizabeth was down at the potato patch, digging. They saw her, a tiny intent figure, stoop to pull up a root and shake it. Judith skipped over to the pantry and began to gather together bits of food: a wedge of mutton and potato pie, some bread, apples. Hannah had seen all this before.

"What are you doing?" she said.

Judith looked at her through narrowed eyes but did not answer.

"Can I come with you?" Hannah asked.

"You don't know where I'm going."

"You're going to the church."

"All right," said Judith after a pause. "Come if you like. But don't interfere."

They came across Major Bartholomew on the sea path. He was perched on a little folding chair, his face shaded by a broad-brimmed hat. His paints and brushes were resting on a board across his lap. When he saw them he placed the board carefully on the grass and stood up.

"Miss Richards," he said, smiling and touching the brim of his hat. "How are you?"

He spoke to Judith, merely nodding at Hannah.

"I'm very well, Major," said Judith. "But, then, no one has been torturing me."

"Oh, please," he said uncomfortably. "I did explain about that…"

"Yes, of course."

"I would like you to know that the minimum force was used. The absolute minimum."

"Well," said Judith, "it wouldn't take much, would it? Not to burn someone's flesh."

"As soon as we saw that it did no good, we stopped. I mean, we did no more than was necessary."

A breeze blew Judith's hair across her face and she swept it out of the way so that she could look straight at him. She was unafraid of him, Hannah saw. You didn't have to be afraid, even of men as important as Major Bartholomew, if you were as pretty and clear-sighted as Judith.

"I do regret it now, I admit," he said, unhooking his glasses and folding them into his tunic pocket. "It had to be done. There are orders, and soldiers must obey orders, but I am sorry now."

He looked at Hannah, as if she might support him.

"As you get older," he told her, "your life fills up with things you don't want to do."

"May I see?" asked Judith, glancing with a cold smile at the picture on the grass.

"It's rather poor, I'm afraid. I'm keen, but not terribly good."

The sisters knelt and looked at the picture. Major Bartholomew stood awkwardly, his hands behind his back, like a boy before his teacher.

"No," said Judith. "It's good. Don't you think so, Hannah?"

"Oh, yes."

She smiled up at the Major, glad to have something pleasant to say to him.

"Well," he said, "the subject matter is so appealing, you know, so calm. The sea and the land together. Suffolk is such a beautiful county."

"Perhaps you should be a painter," said Judith. "Instead of a soldier. Then people wouldn't tell you to do things you don't want to do."

He gave a little laugh and shook his head. "Alas, it's not as simple as that."

"Do you know what you've been painting?"

"Well, it's supposed to be that stretch of coast…"

"It's the place where the creature came out of the sea," said Judith.

"Oh. I'm sorry. I didn't realize…"

"I don't mind, Major Bartholomew. As you said, it's all so calm."

"You must think me very insensitive. I didn't think…"

"Really, it doesn't matter to me," Judith assured him, then added shortly, "What will happen now?"

"About the monster?"

"If that's what you call it."

"I'm afraid I don't know. We've reached something of a stalemate, it seems. We can't go into the church, and your rector friend can't bring it … the creature out. Sanctuary, you see. In fact, it doesn't worry me very much."

"Really?"

"I mean, while the monster stays in the church, it's out of harm's way. If it is a threat, it's been contained."

Judith gave him her cool smile again.

"So you don't have to think about it any more?"

"That's right, Miss Richards," he said steadily. "I don't have to think about it any more."

There was another folding chair outside the church porch. Mrs Corbiss had placed it beneath the yew tree and was sitting in it now, her hands folded in her lap, her chin on her chest, dozing. David and another boy were lounging on the grass playing a game of five-stones.

"Look at her," said Judith as they came up the path. "Sitting there like Guy Fawkes."

David scrambled to his feet when he saw them coming. He set himself between them and the porch.

"What's up?" he asked Hannah.

"We want to go in."

"In the church?"

He looked nervously at the other boy who in turn looked at his own boots.

"Of course in the church, David," said Hannah. "What did you think?"

"You can't … you can't do nothing in there, Han. You said you wouldn't…"

"I don't want to do anything," she answered quickly. "I just want to go in with Judith."

"Oh."

"We're to stop people going in and out," mumbled David's companion.

"What? Just the two of you?" asked Judith.

"And Mrs Corbiss," David said with a nod in the old woman's direction. "But the others'll be back soon. They're only round at The Hat and Feathers."

"We could go in by the other door."

"You couldn't. Dad's watching that."

"Then we've got no choice," said Hannah. "We'll have to go in this way."

She walked straight at David and he stepped tamely aside.

"Well," said Judith when they reached the door, "you made short work of him, Han."

"You be careful, you two," David called after them. "Don't say I didn't warn you."

Hannah's triumph was short-lived. They were at the church door, and the monster was somewhere on the other side. Judith did not seem to be at all bothered by this, but Hannah hesitated. She pictured the monster slumped against the wall by the door. She saw them stepping inside, and a crooked claw snaking out at them. Grabbing at their ankles from out of the gloom.

"Come on, then," said Judith. "Let's go in."

She lifted the catch and pulled the door open. Silence met them. As they entered, a black shape came flapping down the aisle towards them. For a second Hannah froze. Then she saw that it was John Underwood in his clerical robes.

"Judith? Is that you?"

"Yes," she said. "I've brought some food and..."

"Water," he cut in urgently. "Have you brought water? The creature is dying for lack of water."

DRY, DRY

The monster was curled up on a slab of marble and wedged between the altar steps and the foot of the pulpit. They knelt quietly beside him. He was half covered by the tarpaulin and lay perfectly still.

No bars between us now, thought Hannah. But she couldn't be afraid. The monster looked too ill to move.

"You see," said the rector, lifting a corner of the tarpaulin. "His skin is cracking. There's very little water in here. Some in the font. I soaked that up in a knapkin and squeezed some drops into his mouth, but—"

"You must have water somewhere," Judith cut in.

"At the Vicarage, yes. I went to fetch some but they wouldn't let me bring it in."

Judith slapped the floor with the flat of her hand.

"Oh, they are so stupid!"

Hannah leaned forward, her cheek against Judith's shoulder, to see better. She saw the grey skin of the monster's neck, crazed and baked like the mud of a dried stream. Only round his eyes, still closed, was there any moisture. Tears, perhaps, blackening his flesh.

Judith unwrapped her cloth and took out the apples. Their skin was wrinkled and dry, too, but there would be sweet juice inside. John Underwood reached for a penknife in his pocket and sliced one of the apples into thin strips. He tried to push a piece into the twisted mouth but still the creature did not move. Judith took the apple from the rector's fingers and smoothed it against cracked skin.

There was a hissing sound, the sound Hannah had first heard on the beach, and a fishy stench rose from the heap. A foul smell from a foul creature. The creature she'd wanted to kill for Daddy's sake. She covered her nose with her hand and winced.

But she knew she didn't want the monster to die now.

Judith wrung her hands and looked desperately at John Underwood.

"There must be something we can do," she said.

"But what? What?"

Hannah thought of the full jug of milk she'd carried up to Judith earlier in the day.

"If only we'd thought to bring the little jug," she said.

"Milk?" said Judith. "Yes, milk would do. Or wine. You must have wine somewhere."

The rector sat back on his heels and frowned.

"Yes," he said thoughtfully. "There is wine, but…"

"But what?"

"Communion wine, Judith. I can't use that…"

"Your God would be offended, you mean?" Judith said angrily.

"It stands for the blood of Christ…"

"And Christ would rather this poor thing died?"

She reached out and took hold of his sleeve, tugging it as she spoke.

"Didn't David do the same in the Bible story? When he was hiding from Saul? Didn't he eat the Holy bread?"

So they brought the wine, and soaked the knapkin. They took turns to bathe the monster's parched flesh with it, Judith and John Underwood and eventually, with trembling fingers, Hannah. Then they covered his head with the knapkin and looked at each other.

The wine was not enough, they knew. Water was what he needed and they would have to find a way of bringing some into the church.

* * *

Mrs Corbiss was waiting for them when they came out.

"You shouldn't be here, Judith," she said. "You're not well, girl."

"I'm well enough, thank you, Mrs Corbiss."

"Shame on you, then. To go in to that evil beast and take your little sister with you. What are you thinking of?"

Judith had no answer for her and for some moments they faced each other on the path in silence. Then Hannah caught sight of movement over the old woman's shoulder. Three or four people were returning from The Hat and Feathers. She recognized the Protheros and Mr Rayner among them. When they saw what was happening they quickened their step.

"We've had visitors while you've been away," said Mrs Corbiss over her shoulder. "Been in to see the beast."

"Oh, have they?" snapped Mr Prothero.

"Old Flap-ears let them in," David said.

Judith looked at him sharply, her blue eyes flashing.

"Who?"

His cheeks grew pink and he looked away.

"You don't talk like that, William's boy," Judith said. "You show some respect."

"And you leave the lad alone," said Mrs Corbiss. "At least he knows right from wrong. Now." She took a breath which lifted her shoulders, and she smiled. "I think it's best for you to get off home, don't you? You're not wanted here."

Judith remained still a brief moment longer and then walked slowly through the group. They fell back to let her pass and Hannah, as she followed her sister, felt their sullen looks against her back. They walked down the path and out of the gate. Then Judith turned left, towards the town.

"Stupid, stupid," she muttered to herself.

"What now?" asked Hannah.

"What now, Han? Now we fetch water like we said we would."

"But, Jude, they won't let us in again."

"They'll have to. If we don't get water to him he'll die. So they'll have to let us in."

They found a bucket by the stable at the back of The Hat and Feathers. Judith swung it up and dipped it in the horse trough. What little water there was, was rimmed with green and layered with dust. But there was enough to fill the bucket.

They carried it between them and marched back to the church. The metal handle cut into Hannah's palm and her arm began to shake. She didn't know whether it was the weight of the water or fear that made her tremble so. When they turned in at the gate, setting the bucket down to rest, she could not bring herself to look up at the crowd.

"They've come back!" someone called in astonishment.

And then she looked. People were ranging themselves across the path to block their way.

"Come on," said Judith, rolling up her sleeve. "They won't stop us."

But there was no parting of the crowd this time. Mrs Corbiss stood dead centre, her arms folded. Someone was steadily drumming the handle of a hoe against the path.

"Hannah," said Mrs Corbiss, "go back and fetch Elizabeth."

Hannah stared back at her, concentrating on the pain in her hand.

"Hannah, go and fetch your sister."

"Elizabeth is busy," Judith answered for her.

"Do as you're told!" shouted Mrs Corbiss, her face creased with rage.

The sound passed through the crowd like a wave, and suddenly they were all shouting. Mr Rayner lifted his boot and kicked out at the bucket. It jerked back between Hannah and Judith, wrenched from their grasp, and they heard it clatter to the path. Water slopped and sparkled on the gravel. Hannah turned to run and there were arms and shouting faces all around her. She covered her head with her hands. Someone pushed Judith and she stumbled backwards and fell.

"Run, Hannah! Run!"

But a hand was gripping her shoulder and something she couldn't see tugged her skirt, swinging her round. The hoe swung through the air above her. She heard it swish.

"Stop that! Stop that at once!"

A voice outside the crowd. And someone running up the path. A different face among the others, shiny with sweat, round glasses flashing with reflected sky.

"Let them go!" shouted Major Bartholomew. "The next one to lay a finger on either of them will answer to me."

The crowd fell silent and stepped back, glowering at him. Judith got to her feet and dusted her skirt with fierce, angry slaps.

Hannah was still kneeling on the path. There was gravel squeezed tight in her fists. The bucket had rolled to a standstill and Major Bartholomew's board and paints were scattered over the grass where he'd thrown them.

He took Hannah by her elbow and helped her up.

"Are you all right?"

She nodded.

"Perhaps you should go home," he said gently.

She didn't trust herself to speak but she looked up at him, squinting into the sun, and shook her head.

* * *

John Underwood cupped Judith's chin in one hand and touched the graze on her cheek-bone.

"What is happening to us all?" he asked quietly. "How could they do such a thing?"

"They do it in God's name," said Judith, wincing.

She twisted her face out of his grasp and moved away from him. For an instant he was left with his hand still raised and a brief look of embarrassment on his face.

"It'll be all right now," she said. "It doesn't hurt that much."

"We were bringing water," Hannah explained. "But they knocked the bucket over and it all spilled."

"Well," he said, "we have a little water now. Look."

He picked up a stone water-bottle from the floor and held it out for them to see.

"I managed to sneak this past William at the other door. It took a sort of lie to do it, of course, but I hardly know truth from false-hood these days."

"Bringing water in is true enough," said Judith. "Surely you can't worry yourself about that."

"I suppose not, but I used to be so certain about what was good and what was bad."

Judith took the bottle from him and began to unscrew the stopper.

"It's not enough," she said. "He's used to a sea of water, and this is only a tiny drop."

"The sea," said John Underwood to himself. "Yes. The sea is where he ought to be. We should take him back."

Judith looked doubtful. She walked over to where the monster lay and stood there looking down at him.

"He's like a visitor. We should look after him. We can't just send him away."

"And we can't leave him to die, Judith, or take him outside to be killed. Can we?"

"No. No, we can't do that."

"So he has to go back to the sea."

She sighed and tilted back her head. When she turned round to them, Hannah saw that her eyes brimmed with tears.

SILENCE

When Hannah and Judith returned to the cottage they found Elizabeth sitting quietly at the kitchen table. In front of her there was a bleached herring box full of potatoes. Her fingers played on the table, mingling crumbs of grey earth and crumbs from the loaf Judith had cut earlier. She smiled when she saw them and immediately began to sweep the crumbs up with the edge of her hand.

"Where have you two been?" she asked, her voice fragile but bright.

"St Peter's," said Judith directly.

"The church? With Mrs Corbiss?"

"No. Inside the church."

"Oh Judith…"

The smile became lines of anxiety and tiredness.

"Don't fret about it, Elizabeth. You can see we're safe, can't you?"

148

"Did you go, too, Hannah?"

"Yes."

Hannah was stung by the look of disappointment on Elizabeth's face.

"Didn't you try to stop her?"

"Don't call me 'her'," said Judith. "And don't take it out on Hannah. She can't tell me what to do, any more than you can."

She was breathing deeply, holding on to the chair back and staring defiantly at Elizabeth. Elizabeth stood up stiffly.

"I don't want you to go near that thing."

"Someone has to help him…"

"Why? Just tell me why?" Elizabeth snapped; then, suddenly lowering her voice again, she asked, "What's happened to your face?"

"Nothing."

"Judith, look at you. How can you tell me you're safe…"

"You can blame Mrs Corbiss for this," said Judith, touching the red mark on her cheekbone. "Her and the others. They'd've torn us apart if it hadn't been for the Major."

"Stop it! Stop it!"

Elizabeth thumped the table with her fist, and the potatoes rumbled in the herring box. She bowed her head and hunched her shoulders. Hannah began to be afraid. This was Elizabeth, who was always so upright and calm. Who was now grinding her fist into the table and stooping over it, her shoulders shaking.

"Why are you doing this to us?" she choked. "Daddy wanted me to look after us. I promised him that we'd be all right and you're doing your best to spoil it."

"No, I'm not. Daddy wouldn't want us to—"

"Don't tell me what he wanted!" Elizabeth shouted.

She jerked her head up, her eyes wide and her teeth clenched. She grabbed at the herring box and wrenched it off the table. It smashed into the chair Judith was holding, and potatoes thudded to the floor and rolled into corners.

"He was my father, too, Judith, and I was the one he asked to look after this family. So don't you dare tell me what he wanted. You're not as special as you think you are, you know."

She pushed the chair out of her way, went quickly to the door, and paused.

"It's too late now," she said, her voice suddenly small. "Do what you like, Judith. I don't care any more. I'm too tired to care."

Then she went outside and slammed the door. They heard her running down the path. And sobbing, faint and tiny and more distant than the cries of the gulls. Hannah and Judith looked at each other and then, without a

150

word, began to pick up the potatoes. It seemed the only thing to do.

At the end of the afternoon Elizabeth returned and busied herself in the kitchen as if nothing had changed. But Hannah knew that it had. Of course it had. She could see the dust on Elizabeth's black skirt, and the red puffy flesh round her eyes.

And she knew that Elizabeth had stopped speaking to them.

"I've come to ask you a question, Major Bartholomew," Hannah said, sitting with her hands clasped in her lap.

She had come to the castle by herself. Judith would not leave the poor sick beast, and the rector would not leave Judith in the church on her own. So they had to trust Hannah to speak to the Major. They had to trust her because it was so important to get his help. And anyway, there was no one else to ask.

She was nervous, certainly, but she didn't mind talking to him. The hardest part of the task was already over: walking through the crowd outside the church. Seeing them stand and stare at her as she pushed open the big door. Hearing the muttered comments behind her back as she moved, scarcely breathing, down the path.

The Major stood at the window of his airy room. He was gazing out over the marshes and twiddling his glasses in his fingers. He didn't speak so she pressed on with what she had rehearsed.

"Do you think the monster is still dangerous?"

"No," he said after a while, "probably not."

"So, if we take him back to the sea, you shouldn't mind."

"I shouldn't?"

"No. You won't have to worry about him any more, will you?"

"True, Hannah. Very true."

He broke away from the window and sank into his chair with a sigh.

"But there will be other things to worry about," he said. "There are always things to worry officers. That's what they're for."

"Mr Underwood asks if you will help us take him to the beach," said Hannah. "The monster, I mean. To send some of your men…"

"Yes, I thought that's what this was about."

"Can you help, then?"

He watched her, with his elbows resting on the desk and his chin on his hands. His glasses dangled from his linked fingers. After a moment he closed his eyes and put the glasses on.

"Why doesn't he ask me himself?"

"He has to stay in the church."

"Yes, of course. And no doubt he thinks I'll

find it harder to say no to you," he said. "But I'm afraid that's exactly what I must do."

"But why?" Hannah asked, shocked.

"Because Ackford is divided over this monster, Hannah. You want it to escape to the sea but almost everyone else wants it dead. I can't afford to take sides against them."

"You took sides when they were trying to hurt us, though."

"I know, I know. But that was jumping in with both feet and not thinking. Not the military way. That was keeping the peace. I'm sorry it had to happen."

"Then why didn't you let them get on with it?"

"I told you – I acted without thinking. And I'd probably do the same again. But you can tell your sister that it would be most unwise to try to take any more water in. It only provokes them."

"We've got a little in already," she said defiantly. "Mr Underwood managed to bring some in."

"Yes, well, I'd rather not know about that…"

"We won't need to, though, if we can get the creature to the sea. All we want is you to send some men when we take him out. To stop them if they…"

"I'm sorry. I can't do that."

"But it'll die, Major Bartholomew."

She was looking directly into the eyes behind the glasses. Straight at him, the way Judith or Mrs Corbiss might have done. He picked a pencil out of a jar and started to scribble on an envelope.

"I don't want that to happen, of course," he said. "But I really can't intervene. I'm sorry."

Hannah got up. She would have to take this message back to the church. Admit that she had failed. And Judith would be fierce and angry about it.

"Thank you," she said, trying to make politeness sound rude. "I have to get back to the church. Thank you for listening to me."

She left him scribbling jagged lines on the back of his envelope.

William saw her coming up the path. He said something to Mrs Corbiss and the old woman shaded her eyes as if she were watching a boat come in. Hannah tried not to hurry. She tried to walk steadily, bunching her fists so that they shouldn't see that she was trembling.

When she got inside the church she leaned her back against the door and let her breath out slowly. She shut her eyes, feeling the blood pulsing in her temples. Opening them again she saw the heavy stone of the pillars and the patches of coloured light across the floor and the pews. She watched the colour edge further into the aisle, and then noticed that the creature had moved, or been moved. He was in the middle of the altar steps, a black heap that reminded her of the cold fire at the cottage.

She looked around for Judith and the rector but could see no sign of them. As she made her way down the aisle, the black shape twitched. But it didn't have the thick folds of the tarpaulin. It was cloth, black cloth with a soft sheen, and emerging from it was a human head with the rector's face, turning to her and blinking.

A shock of cold ran through her as she realized her mistake. And now she could see that the creature was still in his place by the pulpit.

"Hannah," said Mr Underwood, getting to his feet and rubbing his hands through his hair. "You're back. What did he say?"

"He said no."

And there was Judith, sitting up in one of the pews.

"No? He can't have said no."

"He did. I'm sorry, Jude. I did my best."

"Oh John," said Judith. "He was our last hope. What can we do now?"

Hannah looked sharply at Judith. John. She'd called him John. As if she'd always called him John.

The rector stood in the aisle, passing his hand over and over his hair. But he didn't answer. He didn't want to put into words what they all knew: that the monster would either die inside the church through lack of water, or be killed in the attempt to get him to the sea.

Hannah slipped into the pew next to Judith and slumped forward on to one of the kneelers. She fixed her eyes on the tall window above the altar. St Peter, elegantly wrapped in a long yellow cloth, walking on the water with pale feet. A small fat-bellied boat behind him.

"What good is that?" she whispered.

What they wanted was to sink their fishman into the sea, under the waves, and all that Peter could offer was walking on water. Kept dry by faith. It was a cruel image and she closed her eyes on it.

She heard the rector lift his voice – "What now, oh Lord? What now?" – but she couldn't tell whether it was a prayer or a shout of frustration. Things are never what they seem. In the dark of her mind she saw John Underwood curled up on the altar steps, looking like the monster, and she remembered Mrs Corbiss's angry cry: "Not one monster. Two monsters have come to Ackford."

She opened her eyes and lifted her head. St Peter was still there, looking down at her impassively. Then she heard herself speak.

"Perhaps there is a way."

Judith rustled in the pew beside her, touched her arm.

"What?" she asked. "What did you say?"

"Two monsters, Jude. Perhaps there is a way."

SWEET WATER

'Let me understand this," said John Underwood. "Say it again, Hannah."

The idea was still a shapeless mist in her
mind, and Hannah had to feel for the words.

"If we wrapped something up ...' she said,
"something in the tarpaulin, perhaps, I
thought it might look like it's the monster."

"It would, it would," said Judith, her face
full of life again. "Don't be so slow, John. A
decoy – surely even you know about decoys."

"Of course I do but we must be careful..."

Judith was hardly paying him any attention.
She kneeled up in the pew, took Hannah's face
in her hands and kissed her loudly on the forehead.

"My clever, clever sister," she said.

Hannah laughed and blushed.

"No, listen, Judith," said the rector. "It is a
good idea but we have to think it out."

He held up his hands with spread fingers, as if he was trying to stop the idea floating away from him. Hannah could see the concentration in his frown. It made her think of her visits to the castle with David; how they'd blundered in without thinking. And why they'd gone there. The colour deepened in her cheeks, but her laughter withered.

"It took three soldiers to carry the poor thing in here," he continued. "How can we carry him out? Had you thought of that, Hannah?"

"I don't know. I only thought of the two monsters."

"But we would have to get him out of the church."

"Couldn't we use a cart?"

"A cart, a cart. Yes."

"Two carts, Jude," John Underwood said.

Jude. Hannah and Elizabeth called her Jude.

"If we want them to believe the decoy is our monster, we have to have two carts. And where are we going to get two carts?"

"Haven't you got one?"

"There's a barrow I use in the garden, yes…"

"There you are, then."

"But we'll have to bring it into the church, won't we? And that won't be easy."

"And the trolley where you keep the hymn

159

books," Hannah added. "Hasn't that got wheels?"

Judith clapped her hands and kissed her again.

"Please, please, let me think."

"You think too slowly, John. We could take him down to the sea tonight…"

"No. No, we mustn't rush this…"

"Yes, we must. We must rush…"

"If we go at it like a bull at a gate and we slip up somewhere, what will happen? The plan won't just go wrong. That poor creature will die."

Judith sat back in her pew and the excitement faded from her face. She glanced at the silent heap by the pulpit.

"Of course," she said after a deep breath. "You're right. We mustn't make mistakes."

John Underwood smiled gently at her.

"Let's get the carts worked out first," he said. "Then think what we should do next."

So they took the hymn books from the trolley and made an untidy pile of them on the floor. The trolley had small wheels but it ran smoothly enough on a flat surface. They tipped it over and the rector set his foot on one of the shelves and pushed. There was a screech of nails and the shelf was wrenched free. He kicked out a second shelf and stood back to see what was left.

"There's room enough for it to take some

sort of burden now," he said, "but it won't go easily over grass."

"We'll use it for the decoy, then," said Judith.

She picked up some of the hymn books.

"We can cover some of these with the tarpaulin."

"This is a strange position for a clergyman to be in," he said and wiped his forehead with the back of his hand. "Breaking church furniture and bundling up hymn books like so much rubbish."

"But it has to be done," said Judith.

"Oh, yes. It has to be done. I don't know what the Bishop would say, though."

"Don't tell him. Confess to God. If he's got any sense he'll forgive you, won't he?"

"Perhaps. I don't know. He might wonder whether I'm leading you astray."

"Don't worry about that," smiled Judith. "If this works we'll come to St Peter's twice a week with our prayer books in our hands and nice little hats on."

He laughed.

"Oh, Jude. I can't imagine you in a nice little hat."

The more they thought about Hannah's idea, the more difficulties they discovered. If they brought the barrow into the church, the crowd outside would grow suspicious. John Underwood said he would have to work among the gravestones, weeding and mowing the long grass, and then he would be able to leave the barrow in the church yard.

"After a day or two they'll get used to seeing it there," he said.

"Two days!" said Hannah, thinking of the creature's grey, cracked skin.

"At least two days, Hannah. Eventually I'll be able to bring it close to the north door. We'll take the creature out that way, and the trolley by the main doors."

But Mrs Corbiss would still be watching. Day and night she'd be out there, waiting.

"If only they'd go away for ten minutes," Judith said. "Ten minutes is all we'd need."

"Then we must make them go away."

"But they won't, John. They sit there like vultures all the time."

And they could think of no solution to this problem. John went off with a sigh to start work in the graveyard. At least that was something, some activity, and not just sitting there talking round and round in circles. Hannah and Judith did what they could to soothe the monster's suffering with the little water they'd managed to smuggle in.

Once or twice the creature moved a little. He dragged a limb weakly over the floor. Hannah heard the leathery scratching of his skin on the stone and flinched.

162

"We haven't got enough water," she told Judith.

"I know, Han. I know."

"I wish Elizabeth was with us."

"She doesn't understand, though, does she?"

"But I wish she did. And I wish she was here to help."

They heard a sound like gravel, tiny pieces of gravel, at one of the windows in the south wall.

"Rain," said Judith in a hushed voice. "It's starting to rain."

It was rain. A faint pattering at first, then damp gusts, and crooked streams running down the dusty glass. A fresh draught sucked under the double doors. Ackford was being doused in sweet rain, but there was only the sound of it inside the church. Wet outside and dry in. No use to them.

The north door banged open and John Underwood stood there, his hair plastered to his forehead, his cloak limp with moisture. Behind him the rain angled down on leaning headstones and dark trees waving in the wind. Judith ran to him and pulled him in with both hands.

"Take your cloak off," she said, fiddling urgently with the catch at his collar.

"Fire," he said.

"Don't say anything. We must cover him

with your cloak."

"I know, Judith. But fire. We can start a fire as well. Everyone runs to put out a fire."

"What are you talking about?"

"Start a fire. Outside. They'll all go to see it, Judith, and then – then we can get out of the church unnoticed. The decoy and the monster!"

The rain beat against the church for the rest of the day and into the night. It could be seen driving in from the sea in columns, like misty giants come to reclaim something from the land. Hannah went outside and lifted her face to it. She let it prickle her cheeks and eyes and run into her open mouth. She didn't care whether the people huddled under the yew tree were staring at her or not. Her skirt would become heavy with water and she would walk back into the church with it.

Pools of water shining on the floor. A soft drumming against the windows. Wet trails to where Judith was kneeling by the monster.

Hannah heard glass break and fall, and looked down the church to see John balanced dangerously on the choir stalls. He had thrust one of the shelves from the trolley through a window. There was a jagged space where a saint's elbow had been. He wedged the plank in the gap and rested it on top of the carved stalls so that water trickled into the pulpit and through to the monster.

More damage to the church, but it was raining inside and out now.

And soon they would have their fire. The old shed against the vestry wall. A conflagration that would set the people of Ackford running. And then John Underwood would take the decoy out, and she and Judith would smuggle the monster down to the sea. And no one would stop them. He would be free and alive; they'd all be free, and it would work.

It will, thought Hannah as she walked back to the cottage with Judith. It will work. It will.

The rain had cleared by the following morning. Hannah and Judith stepped out of the kitchen into a yard which had been washed clean. The cottage looked empty to Hannah when she looked back at it, though she knew that Elizabeth was still asleep inside.

"Come on," said Judith. "She won't want to see us."

They set off for the church through long grass which steamed in the fresh sun. When they got there they found that the creature had revived a little. He even took some fish when Judith held it out to him, rolling his boulder-like head to look at her.

"Han," she said softly. "See his eyes? Do you think he knows me?"

"I think he might," Hannah said.

But it was impossible to tell. The creature turned stiffly away from them and stared at the stone step in front of his face. He seemed to stare hard, to study the grain of the stone and every tiny indentation.

But he's trying to see something else, Hannah thought. Not the step but something far away.

There was a noise at the north door and John Underwood came in from tidying the graves. He was wearing an old shirt without a collar and thick grey trousers. It was the first time they'd seen him in anything other than his priest's clothes and he looked sturdier, more boyish. He stamped his boots inside the door and then, seeing the quiet little group by the pulpit – one standing, one kneeling, one lying – he came to join them.

"The water's not enough," he said after a while.

"What do you mean?" asked Hannah. "He's better, isn't he?"

"A little better, yes, but not for long, I'm afraid. He needs more than just water."

"He's languishing," Judith said, sitting back on her heels. "Like Elizabeth."

"Elizabeth?"

"She was in bed when we went back yesterday evening and she was still asleep when we came out this morning."

"Well," he said, "she's had a lot to do these

last few days…"

"It isn't that. Elizabeth was always first up in the morning, no matter what. Now she doesn't care."

Because of us, Hannah thought. She hates us now for what we're doing.

"I liked it better when she tried to boss me," Judith said hopelessly.

John Underwood thrust his hands in his pockets and moved away from them, leaning against a pillar and looking out at the graves.

"Perhaps you ought to stay with her for a while," he said. "I mean, not come up here…"

"What good will that do?" said Judith. "Nothing will be right in Ackford till this poor creature's returned to the sea. We can't leave now."

She went over to him and put her arm through his.

"We can't wait much longer, John."

"Tonight, then," he said shortly. "Why don't we try tonight?"

A BREATH BENEATH THE WIND

Hannah made her way down the gravel path towards the gate. The rain had returned for a spell during the afternoon and the smell of it, sweet and rich and earthy, filled the night air. The moon was low in a purple sky, and the last rags of cloud were clearing fast on the landward horizon. A cool breeze rattled the tops of the trees.

Someone called her name, but she carried on walking.

"Hannah, wait."

Footsteps on the gravel behind her, magnified by the night. She turned and saw Mrs Corbiss detach herself from the shadows, her shawl pulled tight over her head. Some distance behind her, coals glowed in an old oil drum. Several red faces were suspended in the dark around it.

"You look tired, girl. Are you?"

Hannah did not answer.

"You know why I'm doing this, don't you? I'm doing it for your daddy. For Elizabeth and for you. Elizabeth knows that. You go home and ask her."

"Elizabeth doesn't talk to me, Mrs Corbiss."

"Because you are too proud, girl," the old woman said gently. "It's no wonder, Hannah, is it? Where's Judith?"

"In the church. She'll be along soon."

"She shouldn't be left in there with that man."

"She won't be long, Mrs Corbiss."

The lined face came closer to her and moonlight fell on it. Triangles of shining grey on the forehead and one cheek.

"You picked the wrong sister to follow, Hannah. You go home and be humble and listen to what Elizabeth says."

"All right, Mrs Corbiss," Hannah said after a pause. "I'll try."

"Good child. You stand up to evil and no harm will come to you."

Hannah forced a smile and continued on her way. She felt the old woman's eyes on her as she passed through the gate. She turned right, for the sea path to the cottages, and was swallowed in darkness. Then she stopped and listened. The footsteps grated quietly away, up towards the church. Hannah turned round and began to run lightly back the way she'd come. Then past the gate and along a low wall. The mass of the church loomed on her left. She stopped again.

Small voices were coming from the people gathered round the oil drum. Someone laughed.

She climbed over the wall and, keeping low, moved silently between the headstones, peering through the dark until she could make out the shape of the old shed. She felt in the folds of her skirt. Her fingers trembled. Then closed on two objects.

A cold key and a box of matches.

The shed door slammed as she ran out. It banged in its warped frame and rattled. They would hear that, surely. They would look up from their glowing coals and ask each other what the noise was.

She crouched behind a slab of stone, someone's last resting-place, and watched. Beneath her hands, she felt chips of marble. She stared hard at the shed.

Nothing. Nothing was happening.

The breeze was stronger now. It was shaking branches, rubbing them against the shed roof. At last she saw a twist of pale smoke rise. It curled upwards, clinging to the church tower before the wind whipped it away. She waited a little longer, listening.

The dry rustle of moving leaves above and, yes, crackling from inside the shed. Then she saw a line of yellow light flickering under the door.

She scrambled up and ran round the corner to the deepest shadow at the west end of the church. Caught her foot. Stumbled on a tufted mound. She felt the grass come up to bruise her chin, and rested there a second.

Someone else lies here, she thought. Some ancient townsman of Ackford, his grave untended, his bones deep in the soil beneath me.

Inside the shed something rumbled and fell. And now the flames broke out. She knew they'd broken out because a sharp line of jerking light cut across the shadow where she lay. She knelt up.

"Help!" she cried.

Her voice was shaky and feeble and smothered by the wind. She called again.

"Help! Help!"

Then ran to the far corner of the church and screamed in the direction of the north door.

"Help! Fire!"

There was shouting. Feet thumping the turf.

A figure, two figures, hurried towards her along the north wall. They were almost on her before she saw them. She lurched sideways and threw herself down as they thundered round the corner. Then she picked herself up

and ran in the direction they'd come from –
towards the north door.

The door stood open and she could see points
of candlelight flickering inside. Almost all the
tall windows were dark, but there was a
spreading glow behind one in the south wall.
As if the saints in the glass were on the move.

John had wheeled the barrow in and tilted
it where the monster lay. He looked over his
shoulder as Hannah ran in.

"Quick!" he shouted. "Take hold of the
handles and lean hard."

She braced herself against the barrow while
he and Judith pushed against the monster's
back.

"Now," he said through his teeth. "Roll
him, Jude. Now!"

They lowered their heads and heaved.
Hannah saw the tarpaulin fold and stretch in
Judith's white hand. The monster's back lifted
a little, then fell back again.

"Again! Now!"

This time they managed to push the sagging
form far enough to roll against the front edge
of the barrow. Hannah was rocked by a
sudden weight which swung the handles up
and away from her. She caught them again
and tensed her whole body. The wheel began
to slip. John scrabbled round on the floor and
made a brake with his foot.

"Pull down on the handles!" he hissed at her. "Pull down, damn you!"

Hannah leant across the barrow as it strained away from her and her feet were lifted from the floor. Suddenly, her face was pressed against the monster's flank. The twined weed-like strands, the dark flesh and the stench. For a second she thought she was going to be sick. Then the barrow sank under her weight, juddered and righted itself.

First there was the clack of the barrow's wooden feet against the floor, then a low, moaning cry, like an echo of the wind outside. The sound ran through the tall spaces of the church and Hannah felt a chill shudder through her body.

"Poor thing," said Judith, laying her hand on the form slumped in the barrow. "Poor thing."

"No time for that," John snapped. "Take a handle, each of you. Can you lift it?"

They could, but only just. He snatched the tarpaulin from the monster's back and flung it aside. Then he snaked ropes over the barrow, tied them nimbly, and helped wheel it to the door. It bumped over the step and on to the path.

"Now, you're on your own. Don't try to rush it. You must keep it level all the way. If it begins to tilt you'll never hold it, and you won't get it up again."

He turned and ran back into the church. The trolley, piled with hymn books, was waiting by the other door. He grabbed up the tarpaulin and spread it over the books. Then he pushed open the double doors and turned to look back at them.

The south and north doors of St Peter's were in a line. They were in most old churches. Daddy had told Hannah they were built like that in case the Devil should ever force his way in. The Devil always moved in straight lines. If he should come in at the south door, he could be let out at the north. She remembered Daddy smiling and squeezing her hand when he told her.

Now both doors stood open and the night air was blowing through. Hannah, twisting her neck painfully, looked out to the moonlit path beyond the porch. She saw John Underwood hesitate in the arched opening. Look at them as if he, too, might be smiling. Then bend his back to the trolley and push it out into the night.

They could only move slowly, stopping for breath and to change their grip every ten paces or so. The path from the north door was a narrow one, not much used, but it sloped gently and the slope did much of the work for them. Most of their efforts went into holding the barrow straight.

Every time they stopped, Hannah glanced back at the church, expecting to see people running after them. All she saw, though, was billowing white smoke blown flat against the purple sky and flecks of black and bright orange dancing through it. Judith hardly looked back at all. Instead she bent close to the monster, straining to hear his sighing breath beneath the wind.

Hannah hoped fervently that somehow he would understand, that he'd know they weren't trying to hurt him.

Bit by bit, they edged their way closer to the sea.

"Pray God he'll be all right," Judith muttered to herself more than once.

Hannah couldn't tell whether she meant John Underwood or the monster.

They squeezed the barrow through the gap in the wall and on to a broader track which dipped under some trees to their right, like a tunnel. The shouting and the roar of the fire became lost in the whistling and groaning of the wind. A little way along this track the ground levelled and they had to push harder. Now they could only struggle on for a count of four before they had to stop. But the darkness was thickened by the overhanging trees, and that made them feel safer.

They began to hear waves crashing on the shore. Up ahead, only a few more paces, the tunnel of trees ended and they could see the clouds race and, between them, stars hanging in the sky.

Then someone shouted from the black avenue behind them.

"Stay where you are!"

Judith looked at Hannah in blank disbelief. "Push, Han! We're nearly there."

But the voice was calling again. And it was coming rapidly towards them. They heaved at the barrow – once, twice more. Then Hannah felt the swish of a body pass by her and David was standing in front of them, a pitchfork held horizontally in front of him, blocking their way.

"You've had it now," he cried, his chest heaving. "You're done for now."

He tightened his grip on the pitchfork and set his feet apart.

"Don't call them, David," Hannah said. "Please don't call them'

"You've changed your tune, haven't you? A while back you wanted the thing killed…"

"I know."

"They got your vicar friend, caught him at the gate, and I can tell you they was wild when they found out what he was up to."

Hannah pictured the hymn books tumbling on to the path in the moonlight. Pages gusting open. Angry faces closing in.

"Is he all right?" she asked.

"He'll live."

"They hit him?" Judith said, stepping forward.

"They had to, didn't they?"

"Why, David?" Hannah said. "Did he fight back?"

"No, but…"

"What?"

"Well, what he was doing and everything…"

"He was trying to save a life, that's all."

"A monster."

"A monster? You come and see him, David. Come and take a proper look."

"I'm not moving."

"You don't have to be scared any more. We aren't."

"I didn't say I was scared."

"Then come and look."

He was silhouetted against the agitated sky and the stars, motionless. But he was thinking. She knew that he was thinking. And in spite of the wind she could hear him breathing.

"We'll bring him closer, David, if you like," she said. "Shall we?"

He didn't move or answer.

They took up the handles and pushed the barrow up to David's feet. They could see his face now. He was looking steadily at Hannah. His jaw was clamped shut and he was forcing himself not to look down at the thing in the barrow.

"What is there to worry about?" Hannah said. "I was wrong to want to harm him, David. He's one of God's creatures and that's all there is to it."

Then, slowly, David began to lower his eyes.

Without David's help they would never have got the barrow beyond the ridge of rough grass at the top of the beach. They were buffeted by the wind and the wheel slurred into sand and stuck. David wriggled underneath, made a back and heaved them free. But then, when they trundled on to the beach, there were the stones.

"It's impossible," Judith called out in a tight voice.

The barrow struck the stones, jolting to a halt or sliding wildly off to one side. They fought it but, halfway to the sea, it wrenched itself free and plunged over on its side. Hannah was thrown to her knees and felt hard edges press into her bones. She looked at the barrow and saw the dark shape inside swell against the ropes.

The sea growled. The monster hissed in pain.

"We can't do no more," gasped David. "Leave it where it is."

"No!" Hannah shouted angrily at him.

"The tide'll come up…"

"We can't wait for that."

"And I can't wait for the others to find us, Han. They'll do for me if they know I helped."

"Then run away and leave us. Go on. Run away!"

He fell back on to the beach and hung his head between his knees. He flicked the dark hair from his eyes and looked up at Hannah. There was hurt and confusion in his face. Well, so there should be, she thought. It was what she intended.

"Leave us, David," she said again to make the hurt more sharp. "If you can't face it, leave us."

Judith was on all fours, feeling among the stones with desperate fingers. Her hair was whipped across her face. Searching for something.

What?

Hannah's heart thumped suddenly. She put her hand to the pocket of her skirt. Nothing there. The watch had gone. Daddy's watch, to keep his memory alive.

"Jude," she shouted. "My watch! I've lost my watch!"

"I'm not looking for that. Don't be so stupid, Han."

"But I've lost it..."

"I don't care! I don't care!" Judith screamed. "I'm looking for stones. A sharp edge. So we can cut him free."

She snatched up stones and flung them

aside. Hannah sank back miserably and let her get on with it. She watched Judith seize one which had been cracked apart – a jagged, flinty blade – and hold it up in triumph. Hannah looked away. She didn't want to know. Judith crawled to the barrow with the stone and began to saw at the ropes.

There was a shout behind them. A thin sound in the booming all around. Somewhere back in the tunnel of trees.

"They're coming," Hannah said dully to herself.

She looked back at David and her anger turned to pity.

"They're coming," she said again, but he sat there helplessly, his eyes unfocussed, hearing nothing. She knelt in front of him.

"It's all right, David. I didn't mean what I said. Go while you've got the chance."

He didn't even look up. She grabbed his elbow and shook him.

"You've done enough for us. Why don't you get away while you can?"

He wiped his nose on his sleeve and looked at her.

"I'm all right where I am," he said.

Judith gave a little cry as the ropes began to fray and twist. Then she sprawled backwards and the barrow fell aside. The monster seemed to spill on to the beach.

It lay there for a moment, before arching its

back and spreading a clawed hand on the stones. Its arm tensed and it began to move.

An anguished crawl down to the water.

People were clattering over the beach towards them. About a dozen murky figures ran and stopped, fanning out in a semi-circle. Hannah got up and turned to face them: the people of Ackford, faceless in the night. And someone else, leaning on a pole and limping down the slope to join them. Moving like a thing with three legs, pushing its way to the front.

"Stand aside, girl."

Hannah stared back at Mrs Corbiss, but she couldn't speak. The whole world had gone wrong, and Daddy's watch was missing. She heard David drag himself to his feet and move to stand beside her. She looked briefly over her shoulder for Judith. Cold air slapped her face and she glimpsed the tumbling silver of a breaking wave.

The monster at the sea's edge.

Water swirling round him.

Judith, motionless, her skirt rippling, her back to the shore.

Mrs Corbiss shouted something else but the words were snatched away. Sounds were jumbled, sometimes there and sometimes drowned in the roar of wind and water. The old woman thrust the pole into the pebbles and pulled herself forward on it. The figures behind her moved down the beach a little.

For a second Hannah heard the pole grind into the pebbles. And a rasping echo somewhere. In the distance somewhere. A rhythmic crunching.

She peered into the dark, towards the sound. Something like a flapping sail was coming along the beach. Pale, wavering, a blurred shadow around it. And the crunching, which came and went in the wind. Feet pounding the stones.

Then she saw. An apron. Elizabeth, running.

It was her figure and her face, but transformed. Wild. Her mouth open, shouting words which were torn away by the wind. But Hannah knew what she was shouting. She was certain of it.

Leave them alone. Don't touch my sisters.

MORNING LIGHT

It was the storm that sent everyone scuttling for shelter. Mrs Corbiss tried for a while to face up to the wind, struggling down the beach to get to where the monster had last been seen. But it was hopeless; the thing was lost somewhere in black waves that gaped and closed like jaws. Then Mr and Mrs Prothero put their arms round her and huddled her off to their cottage.

Elizabeth held Hannah by her shoulders and shouted at her, but all that could be heard was the booming of the storm and the crashing of waves. She waved an arm in the direction of the church and Hannah nodded. Then she turned into the wind and stretched out her arms to Judith.

As soon as they lifted the latch, the north door flew open and torn branches and shreds of grass blew in around their feet. They put their shoulders to the door, the three of them, and forced it shut. Then the wind was outside, its roar reduced to low moaning or to whining in the tall spaces. Two iron chandeliers were swinging above their heads.

John Underwood was sitting propped against a pillar, one foot stuck out in front and the other folded awkwardly under him. His head was lolling on his chest. Judith ran to him and took his hands. He lifted his head and she saw blood dried around his mouth. One eye was closed and swollen. Raw pink tinged with blue, like the bud of a lily waiting to flower.

"Judith?" he said softly. "Did he get away?"

Nobody saw the monster leave.

Waves smashed on to the shore, again and again; great falling walls of water. No human could have survived that terrible beating – but, as people reminded each other, the monster was not human.

At dawn, when the storm had finished with Ackford, David went down to look at the beach. He went to get away from everyone else – he didn't expect to find anything – and he was relieved when he saw that he had the place to himself. The whole stretch of coast to the spur, north of the cottages was empty. Grey and empty. It was as if the events of last night had been wiped away. In fact, he did find something. He came across the wheel of the barrow and one splintered board, half covered with stones. He stood there staring at them, remembering, and he turned them over with his boot. Beneath the board the stones were glistening wet. One was round, a perfect round, and silver.

He stooped. Not a stone. A watch, face down. He put it to his ear and heard its faint tick. Then he slipped it in his pocket.

So this little thing survived the storm, he thought. Maybe the monster did too.

"I'll take it to Hannah," he said to himself. "It might cheer her up."

He'd give it to her when he saw her. Or, maybe, he'd just wrap it in some paper and leave it at the cottage door.

When he looked up again he noticed that the sea had changed. It was no longer a blue-green sleepy thing, and had become, instead, thick and dull as metal. Broken and complaining, blurring the distance and stinging his eyes with spray.

I've done with this place now, he thought. I could be out there, over the sea. I'm a sturdy lad for my age. If this war gets going, they might take me for a soldier.

After a while he picked up the board and sent it spinning into the breakers. Then he sat with his arms round his knees and watched it bob and swirl among the waves until he lost sight of it.

"I woke up late," Elizabeth was saying, "and I knew you'd gone. I could tell; the place had a desolate kind of feel to it. But I didn't care and I didn't bother to get up. There was nothing to get up for. So I went to sleep again and I slept until it was dark."

She was sitting on the stone floor with Hannah's head on her lap. Hannah held her hand and stared at St Peter on the high window, white-faced, treading delicately on the water. The morning light had gradually brought the colours to life. Hannah turned her head and saw Judith dabbing at John Underwood's eye with her handkerchief, scolding him gently when he recoiled.

"I was dreaming about Daddy," Elizabeth went on. "He was standing in a boat in Ackford harbour, trying to reach the side with an oar. He kept hitting the oar against the side of the boat, and I woke up again and heard the landing window banging in the wind.

"When I got up to close it, I saw a glow up at the church and smoke, and it frightened me. I thought they were trying to burn the monster out and that you were trapped inside."

"It wasn't the church," Hannah said. "It was the shed. I set fire to it."

"I know that now, but I didn't then. I was frightened. Frightened for your lives. So I came running straight up here."

"And found me," said John Underwood with a painful smile. "Collapsed on a pile of old hymn books."

"I helped him inside and he told me what you were trying to do. I didn't care about the monster. What mattered was that you should be alive, not that the monster should die. It took the fright of seeing that fire to show me that. I just knew I had to make sure you were all right. I ran down to the beach, but to the wrong part. I had to turn back and keep going till I found you."

"And you did find us," said Hannah, moving her cheek against Elizabeth's apron. "And you saved us."

"I don't know. The storm saved you, I think."

"The storm saved him," said Judith sadly. "The storm came and took him away."

Hannah squeezed Elizabeth's hand, hoping fiercely that it might be true.

Let him survive, she thought. Let him be out there somewhere.

But she was very tired, and she feared that the hope would not be strong enough. Her eyes began to close. She felt a tear spill on to Elizabeth's apron. And she was falling asleep, thinking about the monster and about Daddy's watch, lost among the stones.

TO TRUST A SOLDIER

Nick Warburton

"The rules of war, Mary. You must promise to keep them or it might be the death of us all."

Sometime in a machine-less future, six soldiers – five volunteers and a professional – are on their way to fight for their country against an invading army when they come across a teenage girl, Mary. She becomes their map, guiding them to the battlefield – or so the men are told by their leader, the flinty, dispassionate Sergeant Talbot, whom they trust as deeply as they distrust Mary. One though, young Hobbs, feels sorry for the girl and a relationship develops between them…

"Warburton has a remarkable gift for realistic writing." *The Times*

BILLY'S DRIFT

Charles Ashton

"Whatever he tried to look at, whatever he tried to think of, it always came back to the one thought: a dog, a dog, a real living dog – a dog of his own..."

This is the story of Billy Stuart. It tells of the hours he spends on the hills, hunting rabbits or in the Bridge Bar on Saturday nights, playing the fruit machine; it tells of the dog he's obsessed by, of his shocking accident and the mysterious events surrounding it. But it's the story too of the narrator Theresa Thain, who, eleven years later, recalls these events and her relationship with Billy. Two stories inextricably linked by the same complex enigma...

This is a compelling and powerful novel by the author of the acclaimed *Jet Smoke and Dragon Fire*.

BARNSTORMERS

David Skipper

"I looked at my friends, but nobody said anything. Nobody had to… We were miles from home, it was Hallowe'en and we were closer to the house of our nightmares than we had ever been in our lives."

The "Barnstormers" are Jack, the story's narrator; tough, rebellious Cal; Tyler, the clown; Kelly, the only girl, and the gang's newest member, Ben. Their den is an old building they call "the Barn". When, one autumn day, Tyler first mentions "the Spook House", scene of an infamous triple murder, no one pays much attention. But Cal's obsession with an old motor bike begins a feud with thuggish Arnie Corman and his gang that sees the Barnstormers undertake a momentous, rites-of-passage expedition along the river. Their destination is the Spook House, where this absorbing tale comes to a thrilling climax.

MORE WALKER PAPERBACKS
For You to Enjoy

☐ 0-7445-3692-8   *To Trust a Soldier*
                  by Nick Warburton   £3.99

☐ 0-7445-3693-6   *Billy's Drift*
                  by Charles Ashton   £3.99

☐ 0-7445-4744-X   *Barnstormers*
                  by David Skipper   £3.99

☐ 0-7445-4741-5   *Jet Smoke and Dragon Fire*
                  by Charles Ashton   £3.99

☐ 0-7445-4742-3   *Into the Spiral*
                  by Charles Ashton   £3.99

☐ 0-7445-4743-1   *The Shining Bridge*
                  by Charles Ashton   £3.99

☐ 0-7445-4350-9   *The Nature of the Beast*
                  by Janni Howker   £3.99

Name _____

Address _____

_____